HAS THE ELUSIVE TAG ELLIOTT FINALLY BEEN CAUGHT?

While matriarch Karen Elliott recuperates at the family's estate in the Hamptons, youngest son Tag is apparently getting down to more than business with his mother's social worker here in N.Y.C.

Seen together strolling through Village galleries, sipping coffees at a Tribeca café and cruising the Hudson, Tag and Renee Williams became the city's hottest couple when they appeared together at a benefit gala last night.

Dubbed the city's "Catch of the Day," handsome Tag was unavailable for comment. Apparently the magazine editor is more comfortable writing the news than making it.

But with their relationship causing quite a stir around town, Tag's grandfather, publishing magnate Patrick Elliott, will no doubt have a lot to say when he returns to town in a few days. Stay tuned!

Dear Reader,

It's February and that means Cupid is ready to shoot his arrow into the hearts of the six couples in this month's Silhouette Desire novels. The first to get struck by love is Teagan Elliott, hero of Brenda Jackson's *Taking Care of Business,* book two of THE ELLIOTTS continuity. Teagan doesn't have romance on his mind when he meets a knock-out social worker…but when the sparks fly between them there's soon little else he can think of.

In *Tempt Me* by Caroline Cross, Cupid doesn't so much as shoot an arrow as tie this hero up in chains. How he got into this predicament…and how he gets himself out is a story not to be missed in this second MEN OF STEELE title. Revenge, not romance, plays a major role in our next two offerings. Kathie DeNosky's THE ILLEGITIMATE HEIRS trilogy continues with a hero hell-bent on making his position as his old flame's new boss a *Reunion of Revenge.* And in *His Wedding-Night Wager* by Katherine Garbera, the first of a new trilogy called WHAT HAPPENS IN VEGAS…, a jilted groom gets the chance to make his runaway bride pay.

Seven years is a long time for Cupid to do his job, but it looks like he might have finally struck a chord with the stranded couple forced to reexamine their past relationship, in Heidi Betts's *Seven-Year Seduction.* And rounding out the month is a special Valentine's Day delivery by author Emily McKay, who makes her Silhouette Desire debut with *Surrogate and Wife.*

Here's hoping romance strikes you this month as you devour these Silhouette Desire books as fast as a box of chocolate hearts!

Best,

Melissa Jeglinski

Melissa Jeglinski
Senior Editor
Silhouette Desire

Please address questions and book requests to:
Silhouette Reader Service
U.S.: 3010 Walden Ave., P.O. Box 1325, Buffalo, NY 14269
Canadian: P.O. Box 609, Fort Erie, Ont. L2A 5X3

BRENDA JACKSON

Taking Care of Business

Published by Silhouette Books
America's Publisher of Contemporary Romance

A special thank-you to the interracial couples that I interviewed who provided the feedback I asked for. It was deeply appreciated and proves that true love is color-blind.

Live happily with the woman you love through the fleeting days of life, for the wife God gives you is your best reward down here for all your earthly toil.
Ecclesiastes 9:9

Special thanks and acknowledgment are given to Brenda Jackson for her contribution to THE ELLIOTTS series.

 SILHOUETTE BOOKS

ISBN 0-373-76705-6

TAKING CARE OF BUSINESS

Copyright © 2006 by Harlequin Books S.A.

Visit Silhouette Books at www.eHarlequin.com

Printed in U.S.A.

Books by Brenda Jackson

Silhouette Desire

Delaney's Desert Sheikh #1473
A Little Dare #1533
Thorn's Challenge #1552
Scandal between the Sheets #1573
*Stone Cold Surrender #1601
*Riding the Storm #1625
*Jared's Counterfeit Fiancée #1654
Strictly Confidential Attraction #1677
*The Chase Is On #1690
Taking Care of Business #1705

*Westmoreland family titles

BRENDA JACKSON

is a die—"heart" romantic who married her childhood
sweetheart and still proudly wears the "going steady"
ring he gave her when she was fifteen. Because she's
always believed in the power of love, Brenda's stories
always have happy endings. In her real-life love story,
Brenda and her husband of thirty-three years live in
Jacksonville, Florida, and have two sons.

A *USA TODAY* bestselling author, Brenda divides her
time between family, writing and working in manage-
ment at a major insurance company. You may write
Brenda at P.O. Box 28267, Jacksonville, Florida, 32226,
by e-mail at WriterBJackson@aol.com or visit her Web
site at www.brendajackson.net.

THE ELLIOTTS

Patrick m. Maeve O'Grady

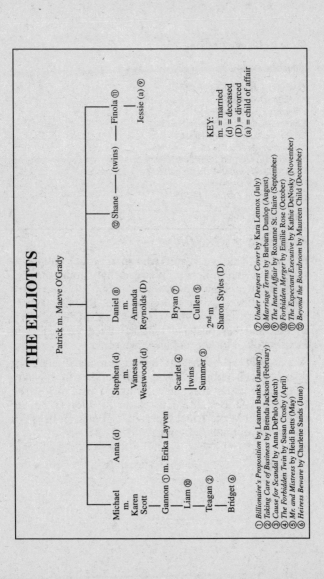

KEY:

m. = married
(d) = deceased
(D) = divorced
(a) = child of affair

① *Billionaire's Proposition* by Leanne Banks (January)
② *Taking Care of Business* by Brenda Jackson (February)
③ *Cause for Scandal* by Anna DePalo (March)
④ *The Forbidden Twin* by Susan Crosby (April)
⑤ *Mr. and Mistress* by Heidi Betts (May)
⑥ *Heiress Beware* by Charlene Sands (June)
⑦ *Under Deepest Cover* by Kara Lennox (July)
⑧ *Marriage Terms* by Barbara Dunlop (August)
⑨ *The Intern Affair* by Roxanne St. Claire (September)
⑩ *Forbidden Merger* by Emilie Rose (October)
⑪ *The Expectant Executive* by Kathie DeNosky (November)
⑫ *Beyond the Boardroom* by Maureen Child (December)

One

"Ms. Williams, Mr. Teagan Elliott is here to see you."

Renee Williams took a deep breath, slipped off her reading glasses and pushed aside the medical report on Karen Elliott, bracing herself to deal with the woman's son, who from what Renee had heard was causing problems.

Since learning of his mother's breast cancer, and trying to assist Karen in dealing with all the paperwork for her upcoming surgery, Teagan Elliott was going about it the wrong way by putting unnecessary pressure on the hospital staff just because his last name was Elliott.

She pressed down the respond button on her phone and said, "Please send him in, Vicki."

Renee silently prayed that her confrontation with him would go well. She didn't want to remember the last time she had taken a stand against a man who thought his last name was the key to open any and all doors.

Her job as a social worker at Manhattan University Hospital meant helping everyone and making sure they were treated fairly, regardless of their economic, educational and cultural backgrounds.

A knock on the door brought Renee's thoughts back to the business at hand. "Come in."

She stood and placed a smile on her face when the man she knew to be Teagan Elliott, of Elliott Publication Holdings, one of the largest magazine conglomerates in the world, walked into her office dressed as if he had just posed for a photo shoot in *GQ* magazine. Renee had to concede he was a handsome man with all the sure-sign characteristics, which included expressive eyes, a symmetrical face, a straight nose and a chiseled jawline.

Moving from around her desk, she met him halfway and offered him her hand in a firm handshake. He automatically took it. "Mr. Elliott?"

"Yes, and you're Ms. Williams, I presume."

His northern accent was polished, refined and spoke of old money and lots of it. "Yes, I am. Would you like to have a seat so we can discuss the matter concerning your mother?"

He frowned. "No, I don't want to sit to discuss anything. I want you to tell me just what will be done for her."

Renee lifted a brow as she stared into the icy blue eyes that were holding hers. So he wanted to be difficult, did he? Well, he would soon discover that when it came to handling difficult people, she could be a force to reckon with. She crossed her arms over her chest. "Suit yourself if you prefer standing, but I've had a rather long and taxing day and I don't intend to stand."

With that, she resumed her seat. The glare he gave her was priceless, and if it weren't for the seriousness of the situation at hand, she would have quirked her lips into a smile. Evidently, not too many people sat down and left him standing.

"Now, about your mother," Renee said after taking a sip of her coffee, which had turned cold. "I see that her surgery is scheduled for—"

"I think I need to apologize."

Renee glanced up, put down her mug and gave him a look. The eyes staring back at her were no longer icy but were now a beautiful shade of clear blue. "Do you?"

"Yes." A smile touched his lips. They were lips that Renee thought were beautifully shaped.

"Normally I'm a likeable guy, but knowing what my mother is going through right now is a little hard to deal with. It wasn't my intent to come across as an arrogant ass. I just want to make sure she's getting the best of everything," he said, coming to take the seat across from Renee.

A part of Renee wondered if there was ever a time an Elliott hadn't gotten the best of everything. "That's what I'm here for, Mr. Elliott. My job is to make sure that not only your mother, but anyone faced with emotional concerns that can impede their recovery is given help to deal with those issues."

He nodded and his smile widened. "Have you met my mother?"

Renee returned his smile. For some reason she was drawn to it. "Yes, I had a chance to talk to her a few days ago. I found her to be a very beautiful person, both inside and out."

He chuckled. "She is that."

Renee could tell Teagan loved his mother very much. In talking with Karen Elliott, Renee had discovered the woman had three sons and a daughter. Teagan, at twenty-nine, was the third child, youngest of the sons, and a news editor at one of the family magazines, *Pulse.* Renee had also discovered during her talk with Karen that of all her children, she and Teagan had the closest relationship.

"So tell me, what are we up against, Ms. Williams?"

Teagan's question broke into Renee's thoughts. "Now that the doctor has given your mother the diagnosis and a decision has been made for surgery, what Karen needs from her family more than anything is support. I understand some of you don't comprehend her reasons for having a double mastectomy when a tumor was found in only one breast. She wants to have both removed as a precaution. Doing so is her choice and should be accepted as such.

"Karen also will need all of your love and support when the surgery is over and during her period of recuperation before she starts her chemotherapy treatments. Again, although there is no sign the cancer has spread to the lymph nodes, she has decided to undergo chemo as a precaution. The outlook at this point is still guarded, but I truly believe everything will work out in your mother's favor since the lump was found early."

Renee leaned back in her chair. Now that it was pretty obvious that Teagan Elliott was just trying to help his mother, although he had approached it in the wrong way, her heart went out to him. It was admirable for a son to care so much for his mother the way he did.

"Do you have any idea when the surgery will take place?" he asked.

"Right now, it's scheduled for next Tuesday."

Teagan sighed as he stood. "I really appreciate you taking the time to explain what the family needs to do. And again I apologize for my earlier attitude."

Renee smiled as she also got to her feet. "You are forgiven. I completely understand how an unexpected medical condition can cause havoc to even the mildest-mannered individual."

He laughed. "I said I'm normally a likeable guy. I never said anything about being mild-mannered."

Renee grinned. Nobody had said anything about him being a handsome hunk, either, but the proof was standing before her. With his six-foot athletic build, jet-black hair and blue eyes, she couldn't help wondering if anyone had ever told him that he bore a marked resemblance to what she perceived would be a younger-looking Pierce Brosnan. He was definitely worth taking a second look at. But she knew a look was all she'd ever take. Men with the kind of money the Elliotts had didn't bother dating people out of their social class. Besides, he was white and she was black.

"Here's my business card, Mr. Elliott. As your mother's social worker, I'm here whenever you need me. Just give me a call."

Teagan accepted the card and placed it in the pocket of his jacket. "I appreciate that. I'll get the family together tonight and we'll talk about what you and I have discussed. Right now my mother's health, as well as her peace of mind, is the most important thing. Thanks for everything."

Renee watched as he turned and walked out of her office.

Teagan, better known to family and friends as Tag, stepped into the elevator, glad he was alone. He released a deep sigh that came all the way from his gut. What the hell had happened to him while in Renee Williams's office? The woman was definitely a beauty, and radiated an almost palpable feminine presence that nearly knocked him to his knees. Nothing like that had ever happened to him before while sharing space with a woman.

When she'd spoken, the silkiness of her voice was enough to stroke everything male inside of him. It had been like a physical caress on his senses. And when their hands had touched in that handshake, it had taken everything he had to control the urge to pull her closer to him. He figured she was about five feet five inches without the pumps, and the outfit she'd been wearing, a tangerine-colored business suit, had definitely defined her curvy figure.

Then there was the coloring of her skin, a creamy color that reminded him of rich caramel. Combined with long, black hair that flowed around her shoulders, and dark brown eyes that had stared at him, she reflected, in addition to striking good looks, compassion, intelligence and spunk.

He actually had to chuckle when he thought of what she had told him when he had initially refused to sit down. Yes, she had spunk, all right, and he would give anything to have the opportunity to get to know her better. But he knew that would be impossible. A romantic involvement with anyone was the last thing he had time for. Since his father had decided, and rightly so, that spending time with Tag's mother was more important than what was going on at the office, Tag was more involved with the magazine than ever. And then there was that blasted challenge his grandfather, Patrick Elliott, had issued that had sparked a rivalry between EPH's top four magazines.

Each of the four magazines was run by one of Patrick's children. There was *Pulse,* the one run by Tag's father, Michael, which was a world-class news magazine; *Snap,* a celebrity magazine run by Tag's uncle Daniel; *Buzz,* which focused on showbiz gossip and was headed by Tag's uncle Shane; and *Charisma,* a fashion magazine run by Tag's aunt Finola.

Last month, Patrick had decreed he was ready to retire and whoever made his or her magazine the biggest success by the end of the year would be given the position of CEO of the entire Elliott Publication Holdings.

When the elevator came to a stop on the bottom floor, Tag couldn't help but look forward to the day his and Renee Williams' paths would cross again.

"So, there you have it, the gist of what the social worker said today," Tag said to his siblings at dinner that evening. The four of them had met at a restaurant in Manhattan, not far from the building that housed the Elliott publications. Gannon, at thirty-three, was second in command to his father at *Pulse*; Liam, at thirty-one, was currently working in the corporate financial department and Bridget, who was twenty-eight, was the photo editor for *Charisma*.

"And you're sure this social worker knows what she's talking about?" Bridget asked, taking a sip of her wine. There was a worried expression on her face. "The decisions Mom has made lately are so unlike her. It's as if she's going to the extreme."

Tag nodded, knowing where his sister was coming from, especially their mother's decision to have a double mastectomy. But all he had to do was recall his meeting earlier that day with Renee Williams to know the woman did know what she was talking about. She seemed very competent and professional…as well as beautiful. The latter seemed to stick out in his mind and he couldn't let go of it. Even now, he couldn't help but remember the smiles he had coaxed out of her after apologizing for his behavior.

"Yes, she knows what she's talking about," he finally said, responding to Bridget's question. "But as I was reminded today, it was Mom's decision to make and what she needs from all of us is our love and support."

Tag felt that he and his siblings always had a rather close relationship, and a crisis such as this was making them that much closer. After thanking the waitress who handed them menus, he turned to his older brother Gannon. Gannon had recently become engaged and Tag, like everyone else, was happy for him. Erika was just what Gannon needed, not to mention, as an editor, an asset to *Pulse*.

"How is Dad holding out?" Tag asked Gannon.

Gannon, who had been studying the menu, glanced up at his youngest brother. "He's doing all right. Today he cancelled an important meeting with a representative from St. John's Distributors to fly with Mom to Syracuse to check on one of her charities there."

"It's hard to believe he's actually putting all work aside," Liam said, shaking his head. All of them knew what a workaholic Michael Elliott was, but even so, they also knew what a strong marriage their parents had.

"That just goes to show how much Mom means to him," Bridget said smiling, touched by the way their father was devoting his time to his wife during her medical crisis.

Bridget glanced over at Tag. "This social worker you met with today. What can you tell us about her?"

Tag leaned back in her chair and smiled. "Her name is Renee Williams. She's African-American, probably about your age. She's very professional and definitely seems to know her business. There is also a calming quality about her that can make anyone feel comforted and reassured."

Liam nodded. "She sounds like just the person Mom needs. This illness has made her spirits decline, and that bothers me more than anything."

That was bothering Tag as well, but he believed Renee could help his mother get through this particular emotional stage. "Ms. Williams is also very beautiful."

The moment the statement left Tag's lips he knew it was a mistake, because it immediately captured the attention of his siblings.

Gannon raised a dark brow at Tag. "Oh, you happened to notice that, did you?"

Bridget and Liam chuckled. Everyone knew how it was with Tag when it came to his interest in women. His mind was spent more on business than romantic pursuits.

Tag knew where his siblings were coming from and smiled. "Yes, I noticed." The last thing he needed was to be thinking about a woman, especially one as good-looking as Renee Williams, but he couldn't help himself. There was just something about her that had touched him on a level that no woman had done before.

"Mmm, the salmon looks good tonight."

Tag glanced over at his sister who was studying her menu. However, his brothers were still staring at him with curious gazes. Uncomfortable with being the center of their attention, he frowned. "Hell, it was just an observation. Don't try and make anything of it."

Gannon laughed. "If you say so, kiddo."

Two

"**M**s. Williams? This is a pleasant surprise."

Renee glanced up from the novel she was reading to gaze into the friendly blue eyes of Teagan Elliott. "Mr. Elliott, how are you?" she said, smiling and adjusting her reading glasses on her nose. "And how is your mother doing?"

She watched his lips thin and a worried look appear in his eyes. "She's not her usual vibrant self and isn't saying a lot about her upcoming surgery to any of us. I talked to Dad and he says it's the same with him."

Renee nodded. "How she's handling things is understandable. Just give her time to come to grips with everything. She has a lot to deal with right now."

Tag shook his head. "I know you're right, but I'm still concerned about her."

"That's understandable. All of you will get through this and so will your mother."

Tag couldn't help but return her smile. Just as he'd told his siblings, Renee Williams had such a calming nature about her. From the first time he had met her a few days ago, he had quickly concluded that she was the perfect advocate for her patients. He knew his mother liked her and spoke highly of her often.

"So, what brings you to Greenwich Village? Do you live close by?" he asked. He had been walking down the street checking out paintings by various artists when he'd happened to spot her in the window seat of the café. At first he hadn't been certain it was she, but then, from the way his body had responded, he'd known for sure. Whether he liked it or not, he was definitely attracted to this woman, and seeing her today wasn't helping matters.

In her office there had been this professional demeanor surrounding her, but here on a Saturday morning, sitting at a window-seat table at a small café and wearing a wool skirt and a blue sweater, she made him even more aware of just how beautiful she was. Even her ponytail didn't detract from that beauty. The temperature was in the upper fifties, one of those inexplicable, rare heat waves that warmed New York in February.

"No, I live in Morningside Heights. I was supposed to meet someone here this morning, but they called at the last minute to cancel. I decided to come here, anyway."

"Oh, I see." Tag couldn't help wondering if the person she'd planned on meeting was a man, then wanted to kick himself for even caring. He quickly decided the blame wasn't all his. He was someone who appreciated beauty and Renee Williams was one of those women whose sultry good looks rang out loud and clear. "Well, I'll let you get back to your reading. I didn't mean to interrupt you."

She tilted her head to the side, her eyes holding his captive. And when she took her tongue to moisten her lips, he found his gaze glued to her mouth. "You didn't interrupt me. In fact, I'm glad I ran into you," she said, giving him a throaty chuckle that did something to his insides.

He gave her a crooked smile. "In that case, do you mind if I join you?"

He could tell she was surprised by his question, but without missing a beat, she said, "No, I don't mind."

As soon as he pulled out a chair, a waiter came to take his order. "Can I get you anything, Mr. Elliott?"

"The usual, Maurice." The man nodded and quickly walked off. Tag looked across the table to find Renee watching him with open curiosity. "Is there anything wrong, Ms. Williams?"

She shook her head, grinning. "No, but I take it that you're a regular here."

His mouth curved into a smile. "Yes, I have a condo in Tribeca and come here often, usually every Saturday morning. I love art and there's nothing like seeing an artist at work." He watched her smile again and wondered if she had any idea how seductive it looked.

"I like art, too. I even dabble in it every now and then."

"Really?"

She laughed. "Yes, really, and when I say *dabble* I mean *dabble*. I've never taken any art classes or anything. I think I just have a knack for it. I believe it was something I inherited from my mother. She was an art major and taught the class at a high school in Ohio."

"Ohio? Is that where you're from?"

"Yes. I even went to college there. Ohio State."

Tag leaned back in his chair. "What brought you to New York?"

Renee sighed deeply. She didn't want to think about Dionne Moore, the man who had broken her heart. After graduating from college she had taken a job at a hospital in Atlanta where she had met Dionne, a cardiologist. She'd thought their relationship was special, solid, until she'd found out that Dionne was having an affair with a nurse behind her back.

What was sad was that while she hadn't known about the other woman, several of the other doctors—friends of Dionne—had known and had been taking bets as to when she would find out. Once she did, it had caused quite a scandal that had had everyone talking for days.

Embarrassed, she had promised to never allow herself to be the hot topic over anyone's breakfast, lunch or dinner table. To repair her heart and put distance between her and Dionne, she had jumped at the chance to relocate to New York when Debbie Massey, her best friend from college, had told her about an opening at Manhattan University Hospital. That had been almost two years ago, and since then she had pretty much kept to herself and had refrained from dating altogether.

"It was a job offer I couldn't refuse and don't regret taking," she finally said. "I love New York."

"So do I."

At that moment they were interrupted when the waiter returned with a tall bottle of beer for Tag. Tag tipped the bottle to his lips, then setting it down on the table looked over at Renee. "So, Ms. Williams, how do you—"

"It would make me feel better if you called me Renee."

"Okay," he said slowly. "And I'd like it if you called me Tag, which is what everyone calls me."

"All right, then, Tag it is."

He glanced at her glass. It was almost empty. "Would you like another drink?"

"No, thank you. The fruit punch here is delicious, but too rich. I'm going to have to do a lot of walking to burn off the calories."

"I'm sorry your date didn't show up."

Renee laughed. "Don't be. It's not the first time Debbie has gotten called away at the last minute. When duty calls, you have to go. She's a friend of mine who works at *Time* magazine."

"Ouch, they're *Pulse*'s strongest competitor."

Renee chuckled. "Yes, that's what I hear."

"But we're definitely better."

Renee reared her head back and laughed. "And of course, I would expect you to make that claim."

Tag took another long pull of his beer. The sound of Renee's laughter was breathy and intimate and he immediately felt a jolt of desire in the pit of his stomach.

He couldn't remember the last time he had allowed himself to unwind, certainly not since his grandfather had challenged the family, sparking everyone's competitive nature. But for once his mind was on something else besides work. It was on a woman. This particular woman. If she could have this sort of effect on him just by being in his presence, he didn't want to think what would happen if he were to touch her. Kiss her. Or better yet, make love to her.

The image slammed into him, sizzling his brain cells and making slow heat flow through every part of his body.

"I guess it's time for me to get up and start browsing the shops."

He glanced over at her, not ready to part ways. "Would you mind if I browse with you? There are a couple of places that are giving private showings today that you might be interested in."

Renee met his gaze. What he hadn't said was that the only way she could attend those showings was with him. The Elliott name carried a lot of weight. She sighed and chewed the inside of her cheek. She had heard about those private art showings and knew that now was her chance to go to one. So why was she hesitating? Browsing the shops and attending a private show or two with Tag wouldn't be so bad as long as she kept things in perspective. She was his mother's social worker and he was being kind. End of story.

She drained the last of her drink before saying, "Are you sure you don't mind me attending those showings with you?"

He placed his beer bottle down. "Yes, I'm sure. I'd like to spend some time with you, anyway."

She licked her lips. "Why?"

He tried not concentrating on her mouth. Instead, he gazed directly into her eyes. "Because I've been working a lot of hours lately and this is the first opportunity I've had to grab time for myself. And because I really enjoy your company."

Her smile was slow but he knew it was also sincere. "Thanks, I'm enjoying your company as well, Tag."

"Then," he said calmly, "that pretty much settles it."

There was a moment of silence, and Renee quickly wondered if anything between them was settled, or just about to get pretty stirred up.

"Oh my goodness, this is simply beautiful."

Tag glanced at the painting Renee was referring to and had to agree. The piece, titled *Colors,* depicted an African-American child standing beneath a rainbow. The artist had been able to vibrantly capture all the colors, including the child's skin tone, as well as the blue-green ocean that served as a backdrop. The happiness that shone on the toddler's face was priceless, and the way the painting was encased in a black wooden frame made all the vivacious colors stand out. "Yes, it is, isn't it."

He picked up the tag attached to the painting and glanced at it. "It's a Malone and the price isn't bad, considering he's making a name for himself now. I was able to purchase several of his paintings at a private art show when he first got started."

Renee could envision the paintings adorning the walls of Tag's condo. Alton Malone, who was of mixed

Caucasian and African-American heritage, had a wide range, but she personally liked his contemporary ethnic paintings the best.

It was obvious Tag liked fine art. But then, so did she. The only difference was that money to buy it came more easily to him than to her.

At the moment, the difference in their incomes wasn't the only thing on her mind. So was the difference in their skin colors. Although New York was one of the most diverse cities on earth, some people's opinions about interracial dating just didn't change. More than once, as they strolled along the sidewalk together, darting in and out of various shops, Renee had felt people's curious eyes on her. Whether accepting or disapproving, she wasn't sure. But the stares had been obvious, as were a few frowns. There was no way Tag hadn't noticed. However, he didn't seem bothered that people were erroneously assuming they were a couple.

"It's four o'clock already," he said. "What about grabbing something to eat before I take you home?"

Renee glanced over at Tag. Earlier, he had asked how she had gotten to Greenwich Village and she had told him that she had ridden the subway. He had offered to drive her home, saying his car wasn't parked too far away. She had graciously declined the offer. Hanging out with him on a lazy Saturday was one thing, but she didn't intend for him to go out of his way to take her home.

"Tag, thanks for the offer, but I'm used to taking the subway wherever I need to go."

"I'm sure you are, but I don't have anything else to

do. Besides, it will be late evening by the time we finish eating."

Renee shook her head as a smile touched her lips. "I wonder when it will dawn on you that I didn't agree to eat with you."

He grinned. "Sure you did. That was our deal, remember?"

Renee lifted a brow as they continued to stroll along the sidewalk. "What deal?"

"Don't you remember?"

She eyed him suspiciously. "No, I do not."

"Then you must be having a senior moment."

"No, I don't think so," Renee said, enjoying this camaraderie with him. "I'm twenty-eight and way too young to have senior moments."

"Not so," he said, teasing Renee. "I'm twenty-nine, but I used to have—"

"Hey, Tag! Wait up!"

Tag and Renee stopped walking when the person called out to him. They turned to see a man—who appeared to be about Tag's age, dressed in a jogging suit and running shoes—trot over to them.

"Hey, man, where have you been keeping yourself?" the man asked Tag when he finally reached them and the two men shook hands. "It's been ages since I've seen you at the club."

"Work has been keeping me busy," Tag said. He then glanced at Renee. "Renee, I want you to meet a friend of mine from college, Thomas Bonner. Thomas, this is Renee Williams."

Renee accepted the man's hand. "It's nice meeting

you, Thomas." She could immediately feel the unfriend-liness in the handshake and watched as he plastered a phony smile on his face.

"Uh, yes, nice meeting you, too." Then, as if she was of little importance, he dismissed her and glanced up at Tag through disapproving eyes. "Evidently, you're not too busy to carve out some colorful playtime."

Renee immediately picked up the censorship in his expression. Evidently, Thomas Bonner thought that she wasn't the type or the color of woman that Tag should be seen with. But his insinuation that she was nothing more than an object of Tag's amusement really got next to her. Breathing deep, she held back her anger, decid-ing this man wasn't worth it. However, Tag evidently disagreed. He placed his hand on the small of her back and eased her closer to him.

She could hear the iciness in his voice when he said, "You should know I'm too serious a guy to ever indulge in playtime. Besides, when a man meets someone this beautiful he doesn't waste his time by acting a fool. If he's smart, he uses it wisely to impress her. And what I'm do-ing, Thomas, is trying to impress. Wish me luck."

Renee could tell Tag's comments left the man at a loss for words. "Uh, well, I'd better continue my run. Give my best to your family," Thomas finally stumbled out before jogging off without looking back. Renee could just imagine the rumors that would be flying around in Tag's social circle tomorrow. Maybe he could handle a scandal, but she could not. She had been there, done that. And she didn't want to ever live through it again.

She glanced up at Tag. "Why did you give him the impression that we're romantically involved?"

The corners of his lips turned up and she hated admitting how much she liked the way his smile seemed to touch his eyes. "Does it bother you that I did?"

She shrugged. "I could handle his comment. He's not the first prejudiced person I've met in my lifetime and he won't be the last. Over the years, I've experienced my fair share of bigotry," she said softly.

"Well, that's one thing I won't tolerate."

She believed him.

They began walking, and neither said anything for a few moments, then Renee decided to break the silence. She glanced over at him. "You never did say why you did it."

Tag sighed. There was no way he was going to tell her that for a moment he hadn't been able to help himself. He had refused to let Thomas think that his intentions toward her—if there had been any—were anything less than honorable. To insinuate that she wasn't someone he could possibly take seriously had hit his last nerve because it was so far from the truth. And that, he quickly concluded, was the crux of his problem. Renee was someone he could take seriously if he was free to engage in a serious relationship. But he wasn't. The situation with his mother was bad enough. Add to that what was happening at Elliott Publication Holdings and it was enough to make a nondrinker order a bottle of gin and guzzle the entire thing.

Knowing that she was waiting for an answer, he decided to give her one. "Thomas was going to think whatever he wanted without any help from me. You're a beautiful woman and I don't consider myself a bad-looking guy, so quite naturally people will assume we're a couple."

"And that doesn't bother you?"

"No, but it evidently bothers you. I learned early in life, Renee, not to care what other people think."

Renee ceased walking and placed a hand firmly on Tag's arm. "And that's probably just one of the many differences in our upbringings. I was raised to care what others think."

Tag nodded. "In this case, with us, now, today, why should it matter?"

She raised her eyes heavenward. Did she have to spell it out for him? It wouldn't matter if it were today or tomorrow. The circumstances would still be the same. "Because I'm black and you're white, Tag."

He smiled, and his eyes sparkled as if he'd just been told something scandalous, simply incredulous. "You're joking," he said in mock surprise. He took her hand, held it up to his, denoting the obvious contrast of their skin coloring. "Really? I hadn't noticed."

She couldn't help but chuckle. And she couldn't help but decide at that moment that she liked him. "Get real."

"I am. And what's real is that I like you and I enjoy your company. This is the most relaxed I've been in a long time, especially since finding out about my mother's cancer and taking on added responsibilities at work. And I'm not about to let a bunch of prejudiced fools decide whom I should or should not date. As for my caring what others think, I've had to deal with people's misconceptions all my life. They think just because my name is Elliott that I've had it easy."

She hated admitting that she'd assumed the same thing. "And you haven't?"

"Far from it. There's no such word as easy with a grandfather like Patrick Elliott."

Renee glanced over at Tag. "Tell me about him."

They had reached the café where Tag had mentioned earlier would be a good place to eat. They sat down right away, the crowd from earlier that day having thinned out.

"Patrick Elliott is one tough old man. He was raised by Irish immigrants who instilled in him a strong work ethic. He worked to put himself through school and because of his keen mind and street smarts, he went to work at a magazine company and eventually founded his own empire."

He paused when the waitress delivered their waters and gave them menus. Renee, who'd evidently been thirsty, took a deep gulp and licked the excess from around her lips. At that moment, a surge of desire hit Tag. It was so overwhelming, he had to briefly look away.

"And?"

He blinked at her single word. "And what?"

She smiled. "You were telling me about your grandfather, but I don't think you were finished."

He chuckled, thinking of how he'd gotten sidetracked. "Oh, yes, where was I?" he said, leaning back in his chair after taking a sip of his own water. "While in Ireland visiting family, he met and fell in love with a young seamstress named Maeve O'Grady. They eventually married and raised many children together. My grandparents have a very loving relationship. However, it's my belief that my grandfather's fear of poverty is what has made him devoted to his business."

Tag paused for a moment, reflecting on what his next words would be. "Although my grandfather dotes a lot on my grandmother, he hasn't always spent a lot of time with his children and grandchildren and isn't very demonstrative, although we all know he loves us. Over the years we've accepted that his true love is his empire, Elliott Publication Holdings, or EPH for short. All of his children are working for the company and he runs a strict ship. He also insists that all family members, including his grandchildren, must earn their way to the top by working their butts off within various levels of the business. No exceptions."

Renee took another sip of water before asking, "How old were you when you began working at the company?"

He smiled, remembering those days. "I was sixteen and started out in the mail room without any special treatment because my last name was Elliott. I later got a degree in journalism from Columbia University."

At that moment, the waitress returned to take their order. They ordered hamburgers, milkshakes and fries. After the woman left, Tag turned to Renee and said, "I don't remember the last time I ate junk food. I'm usually too busy."

Renee looked surprised. "You're kidding. Most people eat junk food because they don't have time for the real thing. So what do you eat?"

"Too much nourishing food. The guy who lives next door to me is a chef and he keeps my refrigerator loaded."

"Jeez, life must be good," Renee said as a smile touched her lips. "Especially since you could call me the microwave queen. I don't have time to cook. I'm so busy, I barely have time to change my clothes after work before tackling some project or another. It's easier for me to just pop a meal in the microwave."

Tag swallowed. Heaven help him, but he could picture her rushing through her house after a long, taxing day at work and taking her clothes off. He wondered how many or how few underthings she wore. He then wanted to kick himself for even letting that speculation rule his thoughts. It wasn't like he was ever going to get involved with her, and needed to know.

"I meant what I said earlier, Tag. You don't have to take me home."

Tag glanced over at her. So they were back to that again, but he was determined to dig in his heels. There was no way he would put her on a subway when it wouldn't be any trouble giving her a ride. "You did say you've met my mother, right?" he asked, looking deep into Renee's eyes.

The blue gaze almost held her spellbound. "Yes. Why?"

"There is one trait she has that you may not have picked up on yet, and of all her children I'm the one who inherited it the most."

Interested, Renee couldn't help but ask, "And what trait is that?"

"Stubbornness."

"Ah," she said, nodding. "And what if I told you that I can probably be just as stubborn as you?"

He studied her a moment before a smile touched his lips. "The only thing I can say is that a standoff between the two of us ought to be very interesting."

Three

"Okay, I concede, Teagan Elliott. You won this round."

She might have to concede on that issue, Tag reasoned, but he personally had to concede that she looked good sitting in his car. "Now come on, Renee. Did you really think the gentleman in me would have you roaming all over New York in the dark?"

She gazed at him in obvious frustration when he brought his vehicle, a Lexus SUV, to a stop at the traffic light. "I don't see why not, since I do it all the time. And riding the subway isn't roaming. It's getting from point A to point B."

Tag couldn't help but shake his head and silently admitted that he had totally enjoyed the time he had spent with her today. It had been clean, honest, wholesome fun. Although he would be the first to admit that developing a relationship with her would be high on any man's agenda, it wasn't on his. Not that he wasn't interested, because he definitely was. He just didn't have the time. *Pulse* was the only thing he was romancing these days. *Pulse,* and his family.

"I live in the next block."

Her voice reined his thoughts back in. "Nice neighborhood. I used to jog a lot in the park while attending Columbia."

She smiled over at him. "I jog there a lot now. I'm a member of the Morningside Park Coalition. We work with the city to preserve and improve the park."

When he came to a stop in front of her apartment building, she said, "You don't have to walk me to the door."

A part of Tag couldn't help wondering if the reason was that she didn't want to be seen with him. For some reason the thought bothered him. He leaned toward her and touched her cheek. "Sorry, there's no way I can deliver you home halfway. My task wouldn't be completed until I walked you to the door and made sure you got into your place okay."

"Thanks. I didn't wanted to put you out." She smiled and he immediately felt her warmth. Relief ran through him that she wasn't uncomfortable being seen with him. Still, he sensed her nervousness. Was she worried that he would try to kiss her goodbye? What if he did? Would she reciprocate? There was only one way to find out.

Renee watched as Tag came around the front of his vehicle to open the door for her. She couldn't help but think about how much difference there was between him and Dionne. Other than the obvious skin coloring, there was the way they regarded women. Because Dionne had been raised by a single mother who'd evidently been a superwoman, he had expected a woman to be able to do just about anything for herself, including opening her own car door and seeing herself into the house. The only time he'd walked her to the door was when he had expected to spend the night.

"Thanks," she said when Tag opened the door and offered his hand to help her out of the vehicle. Her heart fluttered at the feel of their hands touching, and she couldn't help wondering if the reaction was one-sided. Evidently it wasn't since he continued to hold her hand while walking her up the steps to her apartment.

He continued to hold her hand while walking her up the steps to her apartment.

He stepped aside while she unlocked the door. She wondered if he was waiting for her to invite him in. All day they had enjoyed being together without any type of flirtation, or promises of getting to know each other better. So why was her heart beating a thousand beats a minute, and why was she feeling heated from the way he was looking at her?

She cleared her throat. "Thanks again, Tag. I really enjoyed today."

"So did I. And bundle up good tonight. I understand the temperature will begin dropping around midnight."

"Okay." She thought of her huge bed where she would be sleeping alone, and for the first time in two years the thought actually bothered her. It also made her realize that Dionne had been the last man she'd been serious about. Once she moved to New York she had spent more time developing her career than seeking out any worthwhile relationships with the opposite sex. She had kept telling herself she was only twenty-eight and there was no rush. Now she suddenly felt... rushed.

"Will you have dinner with me tomorrow night?"

She blinked, then gazed into Tag's piercing blue eyes. She swallowed the thickness in her throat. "Dinner?"

"Yes, dinner. Tomorrow night."

Renee sighed. Okay, he had asked the million-dollar question, so how would she respond? She had to be honest with herself. If he had been an African-American male she would probably not have hesitated, but there were issues she needed to consider with him being white. The difference in their race was a major factor, but then so was the difference in their social backgrounds. His family owned a magazine publishing company whose headquarters took up an entire Manhattan block, for crying out loud. He lived in Tribeca of all places. An area known for its high-rise condos, quiet streets, good schools and wealthy lifestyles. It was a haven for the well-to-do. For people like the Elliotts.

"Renee?"

She glanced over at him. "Yes?"

"Can we step into your apartment to finish this conversation? I think we're drawing unwanted attention."

Renee glanced around, noting his statement was true. A couple of people in her apartment building were openly staring at them. She returned her gaze to his. "Yes, let's go inside."

She opened the door, and the moment they stepped over the threshold, heat filled her insides in a way it hadn't ever before. "Can I get you something to drink?"

He leaned back against her closed door, placing his hands in the pockets of his jeans. "No, I'm fine, but what you can do is give me an answer to my question about dinner tomorrow night."

Renee nervously licked her lips.

"Don't do that."

"Do what?"

"Lick your lips like that. You've done it several times today and each time I've wanted to replace your tongue with my own. Even now I'm standing here fighting the urge not to."

His words fanned an already heated spot deep within her. Her heart suddenly began beating faster. Out of habit she automatically licked her lips again and when she realized what she'd done, she quickly said, "Oops. I didn't mean to do that."

His eyes stayed glued to her face. "Too late. It's been done."

He slowly moved away from the door, removing the distance separating them. When he came to a stop in front of her he studied her with an intensity that she felt all the way to her toes.

"This is crazy," he said in a deep, husky voice, "but I'm dying to kiss you."

Yes, it *was* crazy, she silently agreed. Because she was dying for him to kiss her. Earlier, she had listed in her mind all the reasons they couldn't become involved, but at that very moment, the only thing she could concentrate on was the way he was looking at her, the heat that seemed to take over her body and the desire that was flowing through her veins. No man had ever made her feel this way before.

He was watching her as carefully as she was watching him. They both knew their next move would be one they wouldn't forget in a long time—if ever. Tag studied her lips, saw them quiver nervously and knew the exact moment she would lick them with her tongue.

He was ready.

His tongue captured hers outside of her mouth, tangled with it as he thoroughly explored all of her, taking this intimate pleasure to a level he had never taken it before. Kissing was a special way to communicate without words, and what they weren't saying was turning him on even more, stirring emotions he had denied himself for so long. Affection, passion and even lust ruled his thoughts, his mind and his body.

He thought her lips were beautifully shaped and her response to him had been spontaneous. He liked her taste, he was drowning in her fragrance and he was taking the kiss to a level he hadn't known was possible.

Renee was literally panting for breath, but the thought of their mouths disconnecting was something she didn't want to think about. She had never been kissed like this before. Tag was taking the art of French kissing to a whole other level. He wasn't just keeping her tongue busy, he was intimately mating with it, leaving her breathless, weak in the knees, moaning out loud. He seemed to be lapping up each and every sound she made.

A part of her brain wanted to shut down everything

she was feeling. It tried reminding her that what they were doing wasn't good. He was white, he was rich, his mother was her patient...and so on and so forth. But at that very moment, the only thing that was getting through to her was the tingling she felt all the way to her toes as well as the pool of heat that had settled right smack between her legs. And there was also the hardness of him that she felt against her thighs, and the sensitive feel of her nipples pressed against his solid chest.

Slowly, he pulled away, drawing in a deep breath. The sound filtered through her like a soft caress. The blue eyes staring at her held such intensity it made her pulse race even faster.

"That," he said softly, "was my first."

She held his gaze, had been drawn into it, was locked into it. "Your first what?" she somehow managed to ask in a tone that sounded like a whisper.

"My first real kiss." His brow furrowed as if he was somewhat troubled at the thought. "I've never given so much of myself to a woman before."

His words touched her in a way she had never been touched before. They were just as deep and profound as his kiss had been. He reached out and lifted her chin with the tip of his finger. "You are simply beautiful." He then shook his head as if amazed. "No, I take that back. You are beautiful. There is nothing simple about it."

He leaned forward and kissed her lips again. "Now to repeat my earlier question, will you have dinner with me tomorrow night?"

Renee released a long, drawn breath. Her mind, thanks to Tag, was jumbled in mass confusion, but the one thing that rang clear was the fact that they shouldn't see each other again this way for a number of reasons on which she didn't want to dwell at the moment. "I don't think having dinner with you is a good idea."

He lifted a dark brow, angled his head and asked, "Why not?"

She sighed deeply. He was making this difficult. What was obvious to her evidently wasn't to him. That kiss had revealed too much. Too many more of those and she would be falling hard and heavy for him, not caring about the differences between them.

Knowing he was waiting on an answer, she decided to take the easy way out. "Your mother is my patient so we shouldn't be getting involved."

Tag opened his mouth to say having dinner with him was not getting involved, but that wouldn't be completely honest. If he were to take her to dinner, he would want to kiss her good-night, and another kiss like the one they'd shared just might have him begging for a taste of something else. When they had kissed, and he had stroked her tongue with his own, her lips had been so soft, her tongue welcoming and her flavor so sweet....

"For how long?" he asked, leaning back against the closed door.

Renee blinked. "How long what?"

"How long will my mother be your patient?"

Renee nervously shoved her hands into the pockets of her skirt. "Officially, until after her surgery and she is released from the hospital. But I'll still be there for her if she needs me once she begins her chemotherapy."

He nodded. "And this rule about not getting involved with your patient's family is yours or the hospital's?"

Renee swallowed. The blue gaze that had her within the intensity of its scope seemed to burn fire wherever it touched. Right now it was on her lips and her mouth was feeling the heat. She nervously licked her lips and saw the moment his stomach clenched and remembered his reaction whenever she did that. "It's mine, but I think it's for the best."

"Do you?" The smile that suddenly appeared at his lips was challenging, sexy and brazen. "Then I guess I'm just going to have to prove it's not for the best, won't I?"

He reached out, gently pulled her close, gave her a hug and then whispered close to her ear, "Stay warm tonight and think about me." And with that he turned and left.

"So how's your weekend going, Tag?"

Tag glanced up from pouring wine into two glasses and met his brother's gaze. Liam had dropped by for a visit but Tag could tell how he'd spent his Saturday was the last thing on his brother's mind; however, he answered anyway. "It was rather nice. I decided to take some time away from work and attended a couple of art shows in the Village."

Liam rubbed his hand down his face. Tired. Frustrated. Agitated. All three. "It's good to know someone can put work on hold for a while to enjoy himself."

"So can you," Tag said, leaning back against the counter. Liam, financial operating officer at EPH, was known as a financial wizard. "Taking time off to rest and relax won't put the company in the red, Liam. Besides, you deserve it."

Liam sighed deeply. "Speaking of putting the company in the red," he said, after taking a sip of his wine, "I'm worried about Granddad's challenge. Personally, I don't see it helping the company. In fact, I see it hurting us in the long run. What on earth could he have been thinking to pit us against each other like this? Yesterday I was walking down the hall and as soon as I turned the corner whatever conversation Aunt Finola and Scarlet were having practically died on their lips when they saw me. It was as if they considered me a spy or something."

Tag nodded at what Liam was saying. He'd encountered a similar situation last week when he'd walked in on a conversation between his uncle Daniel and his cousin Summer. It was weird how everyone had begun acting all secretive because of his grandfather's challenge.

"Granddad is a smart man," Tag said. "Although I don't understand why he would do such a thing, I have to believe he'd never do anything that would eventually hurt the company. You know how he feels about it. It's his baby."

Liam, grudgingly, had to agree. "So, are you ready for Tuesday?" he asked, taking another sip of wine.

Tag shook his head. Tuesday was the day their mother was scheduled for surgery. "No, but the sooner Mom gets it over with, the sooner she can get better."

Liam closed his eyes for a moment in sheer exhaustion. "Yes, you're right." He then checked his watch and stood. "I think I'm going to stop by the office and finish up a couple of things before going home."

After Liam left, with nothing else to do, Tag showered and got ready for bed. The moment he crawled under the covers he thought about Renee. He hadn't meant to kiss her but he had and that had been the beginning of his problem.

He hadn't expected to develop a taste for her, but he'd done that as well. He had wanted to keep on kissing her, tasting her, mating their mouths. To keep indulging. Her lips had felt warm beneath his. Warm and heated with a surrender she hadn't wanted to make but he had coaxed out of her anyway, each and every time he had lowered his mouth to hers.

And earlier today, while with her in Greenwich Village, they had talked about a number of things. She had shared with him that her parents were both deceased. When she was ten years old her father had died of a work-related injury, and her mother had died of colon cancer when Renee was in her last year of high school. She had remembered how kind the social workers and hospital staff had been to her and her mother, and eventually followed in their footsteps, obtaining a degree in social work, with a specialty in health services.

During the time they had spent together today, he had watched her and had been touched at how the smallest thing could make her smile. He'd watched how she interacted with people in general; always respectful, courteous, polite and considerate. Even when she hadn't needed to be…like with Thomas Bonner.

The man had seen something in Renee that Tag hadn't. Color. To Tag, Renee was a beautiful woman. He didn't see her as a woman of a particular skin tone but as a desirable woman he wanted. But he had a feeling it hadn't been the same with her. He had seen the same frowns, stares and censored expressions that she had today. However, while he'd merely chalked them up to ignorance, he could tell they had bothered Renee. All day with her he'd assumed they were developing a friendship. But after kissing her, tasting her, he wanted more. He wanted something he hadn't thought about sharing in a long time with a woman. He wanted a relationship.

Damn.

How could he decide something like that after spending one day with her? Sharing one kiss? He wasn't sure just how deep he wanted the relationship to go but he did know that he wanted one. He wanted to take her out to dinner, the movies, and the theater…just to name a few places. He wanted to show up at her apartment some afternoons and discuss how his day had gone and hear how hers had gone as well. He wanted to invite her over to his place and cook for her…or have Lewis, his friendly chef next door, do the cooking. And he would love taking her to Une Nuit, his cousin Bryan's restaurant, and introducing her to his entire family.

He shook his head and sighed deeply. He'd never thought about introducing any woman to his family before, but he wanted to do it with Renee. He wanted to share all things with her.

He ran his hand down his face, frustrated, because she didn't want any of that. He knew he had to give her time, space and not rush her. Not only would they be engaging in an affair, but it would be an interracial one.

At least that was probably how she would see it. He saw it as simply a man and woman who were attracted to each other deciding to take it to the next level.

But that had to wait. Right now, he had to be content to see her on Tuesday at the hospital. Somehow, though, that wasn't good enough.

Four

"**Y**our wife's surgery was a success, Mr. Elliott."

Tag could see profound relief on his father's face as well as on the faces of his siblings gathered in the waiting room. "And you think that you got it all?" Michael Elliott asked.

Dr. Chaney nodded. "Yes, although her condition will still be guarded for a while, I believe we got all the cancer. She will remain here for a few days, and then I'll release her to you for convalescent care."

"How soon can we see her?" Gannon asked with his fiancée by his side.

"Not for a while yet, possibly an hour or so. She was put under heavy sedation and is still in the recovery room. I suggest all of you go grab a bite to eat. When you come back, she should be awake."

After the doctor left, Michael met his offspring's intense gazes. "Your mother is going to be fine now. When she's released I'm taking her to The Tides to recuperate."

Tag nodded. The Tides was the Elliott family's five-acre estate on Long Island. His grandfather had purchased the estate forty years ago when he became successful and had moved his young family out to the island because the area had reminded Tag's grandmother of her Irish homeland. It sat on a bluff like a fortress and overlooked the Atlantic Ocean. Tag agreed it would be the perfect place for his mother to rest, relax and heal.

"I like your mother's social worker," Michael Elliott said. "It was nice of her to drop by and check on us earlier."

Tag's head snapped up. "Renee was here?" He noticed the way his father looked at him, probably surprised with his use of the woman's first name, indicating some personal familiarity.

"Yes, she dropped by an hour or so ago, when you, Gannon and Liam had left to go downstairs for coffee."

Tag nodded, absorbing that statement silently. He wished he had been there when she'd shown up. He checked his watch, making a quick decision. "Since Dr. Chaney said it will be at least another hour before any of us can see Mom, I think I'm going to walk around a bit." He glanced over at his brothers and their expressions clearly said, *Walk around? Yeah, right.*

Ignoring them, Tag excused himself and headed for the nearest elevator.

* * *

"Is it true that you're Karen Elliott's social worker?"

Renee glanced up from her sandwich and met Diane Carter's curious gaze. Diane was a trauma nurse and one of the hospital's worse gossips. She was quick to get upset if someone got into her business yet she made it a point to get into everyone else's. Usually Renee avoided the woman at all cost but every once in a while she would join Diane for lunch when no one else would.

Renee had to concede that with Diane's blond hair and blue eyes she was a natural-born beauty. But rumor had it that besides having a problem with loose lips, she also had a tendency to be too clingy, which turned off a lot of the men in whom she'd shown interest.

"Yes, I'm Karen Elliott's social worker," Renee finally said after taking a sip of her lemonade.

"Boy, aren't you the lucky one," Diane said with a smirk. "Have you met her sons?"

Renee thought about Tag. "I've met only one. Teagan Elliott."

"And what do you think of him?"

The last thing Renee would do was tell Diane what she really thought of Tag. "He's okay."

Diane leaned back and looked at her like she definitely had a few screws loose. "Just okay? I've seen photographs of him in the society section of the newspaper a few times and he's so handsome he makes your eyes ache."

No sooner had Diane's words left her lips, Renee's hand froze on the glass of lemonade she was about to bring to her lips when Tag walked into the hospital's café. He glanced around as if he was looking for some-one, then his eyes lit onto her.

The connection of their gazes did funny things to Re-nee's insides. It didn't take much to remember the kiss they had shared three days ago; a kiss that still heated her all over whenever she thought about it.

"Renee, are you all right?"

She quickly looked at Diane. No, she wasn't all right, but Diane would be the last person she would tell why. "Yes, I'm fine." And with as much effort as she could muster, she took a sip of her lemonade then bit into her sandwich, trying not to notice that Tag was standing across the room staring at her.

Tag sucked in a deep breath the moment his gaze slammed into Renee's. He wanted her. How could he not? Why had he thought for one moment that he'd con-vinced himself he could not get involved with her or anyone because he didn't have the time? Who was he kidding? He definitely wanted to get involved when the object of his attraction was Renee.

He drew in a deep breath of air as he began making his way across the room. He had gone to her office and was told by her secretary that she was at lunch and chances were he would find her in the cafeteria. He had hoped she would be alone but it seemed she was dining with someone. But that didn't stop him from wanting to see her, talk to her.

Renee hadn't realized that Tag had crossed the room until he was standing right next to her table. She glanced up and felt the sensuous undercurrents automatically radiating between them and wondered if Diane noticed them too.

Immediately putting her professional facade in place Renee leaned back in her chair, cleared her throat and in her best businesslike voice, said, "Mr. Elliott, how are you? And how is your mother?"

Tag sensed her nervousness, saw the guarded look in her eyes and watched how she caught her bottom lip between her teeth. He gave her companion no more than a cursory glance, but quickly registered how she eyed him with keen interest. He knew what Renee was silently asking him.

"My mother is fine, Ms. Williams," he said in his own businesslike voice. "Her doctor indicates the surgery was a success. However, that's what I want to talk to you about and I hate to intrude on your lunchtime, but I was wondering if I could speak with you privately for a moment."

Renee felt Diane's eyes on them, taking it all in, and was glad Tag had picked up on her silent warning. The last thing she needed was for the nurse to start rumors floating around the hospital. "Yes, I was finished here anyway. We can go back to my office."

Feeling a gentle kick to her leg under the table, Renee realized Diane was eager for her to make introductions. "Mr. Elliott, I would like for you to meet Diane Carter. She's one of our trauma nurses."

Diane was beaming when she presented Tag her hand. "Mr. Elliott, it's so nice meeting you."

"The same here, Ms. Carter. I hate to take her away from you, but there is this pressing matter I need to discuss with her."

Diane waved off his apology. "Hey, there's no reason to apologize. Trust me, I understand."

Reneé doubted that Diane really did when she herself didn't.

Warmth spread through Renee's veins the moment she and Tag stepped into the elevator together. Alone. Neither of them said anything and as they rode up to the sixth floor, she tried to remind herself of all the reasons they could not become involved.

"I'm sorry I missed you earlier when you came to see how my family was holding up."

"It's part of my job to check on the family of my patients during surgery, to see if there's anything I can do for them."

Tag leaned against the paneled wall. "That's good to know, since there is definitely something you can do for me."

"And what can I do for you, Mr. Elliott?"

"For starters, since we're alone now, you can stop pretending Saturday night never happened. That we never kissed. Touched. Lost our heads and minds to passion."

He heard the air when it suddenly rushed from her lungs. He saw the shiver that passed through her body, but before he could make another comment, the elevator came to a stop.

When the door slid open, Tag stood back to let Renee step out. Neither said anything as they crossed the lobby to her office, walking side by side. Her secretary looked up and smiled before returning her attention to her computer. Renee appreciated the fifty-something woman who had been her secretary for the nearly two years Renee had worked there. Vicki was efficient, trustworthy and someone who respected Renee's need for privacy.

Renee opened the door and stepped into her office. Tag followed and closed the door behind them. He watched as she quickly crossed the room, and couldn't help but admire how she looked in her chocolate-brown business suit. The skirt hit her just above her knees, and his first thought was that she definitely had a great pair of legs.

"I'm glad you mother's surgery was successful."

Tag's gaze moved from her legs to her face. She was standing in the middle of her office, eyeing him nervously. "So am I."

She cleared her throat again. "In the cafeteria you said you needed to talk to me about her."

He shrugged, deciding to be completely honest with her. "It was something I said to get you alone."

He watched her eyes narrow. Okay, so she wasn't happy hearing the truth, but seeing her standing here, alone in the room with him, made him realize the lie had been worth it. He smiled.

Renee wished she could somehow banish the sight of Tag standing there dressed in a tailored suit, like he was the epitome of every woman's fancy. But then she had to quickly concede that he could have been dressed in a T-shirt and a pair of tattered jeans and he still would have looked good.

And then there was the way his mouth could curve

into a smile. The way it just did. She swallowed. "Mr. Elliott, I'm going to have to treat this strictly as a business meeting."

"If you'd like."

Renee was becoming frustrated and Tag wasn't helping matters. "I have a job to do."

He leaned back against the door and chuckled. "You don't have to remind me since your job is what brought us together."

"We aren't together."

"It depends on your definition of the word," he said easily.

Deciding enough words had been said, he moved forward, closing the distance between them, and came to a stop in front of her. "I need to get back. My mother should be coming around and I want to be there when she does." He paused briefly and then added, "But I wanted to see you, just to assure myself that Saturday had been real and not a pleasant figment of my imagination."

Renee crossed her arms over her chest and lifted her chin. "So what if it was real? That was then and now is now. I should not have let things get out of hand like that."

"You sure about that?" Tag asked. He wanted to kiss that lie right off her mouth. There was no way she could convince him that she regretted what they'd shared Saturday.

"Yes, I'm sure."

"And you don't want me to kiss you again?"

"Absolutely not! I wish you'd never kissed me in the first place!" Renee glared at him and noticed his eyes seemed more intense than ever. She sucked in a deep breath when he leaned down and brought his mouth close to hers, mere inches away.

"Now tell me again that you wish we'd never kissed," he whispered hotly against her lips.

Renee opened her mouth to say the words and had planned to come up with a comeback that would set him back a notch. But she couldn't make the words come out and quickly closed her mouth. She gazed at the face so close to hers and knew frustration, want, desire as she felt herself being pulled in, falling helplessly into the depths of his bottomless sea-blue eyes.

"Tell me," he whispered against her lips.

She inhaled deeply as a throbbing sensation took over her body that seemed to start in the nipples of her breasts and was slowly moving down past her waist to land right in the middle between her thighs.

This was not supposed to be happening to her. She'd never been drawn to a man this way. And she had always stayed within what she'd considered her comfort zone while dating. Although she'd accumulated a number of white male friends over the years, she'd never given thought to developing a serious relationship with any of them. But there was something about Tag that defied logic. Her logic anyway. He seemed to find her as sexually appealing as she found him.

And she wanted to kiss him again.

Knowing that she would regret her decision, she tilted her chin which brought their mouths closer. But he didn't move. Instead he stood there, cool as you please, his gaze holding hers while sending delectable shivers down her body. The shivers, combined with the racing of her heart, were having one hell of an effect on her. But still he stood there, immobile, letting her know that if she wanted the kiss she was going to have to be the one to take it. With a moan she hadn't known she was about to make, against her better judgment she leaned closer and captured his mouth with hers.

She grabbed his shoulders and welcomed his tongue when it entered her mouth, mating it with hers, stroking it and sending tremors of pleasure through her body.

Then the tempo of the kiss changed when he took it over. It went from soft and gentle to hot and possessive. And she responded automatically, feeling her abdominal muscles clench. Intense heat pooled between her legs and the scent of all male teased her nostrils.

The ringing of the phone intruded and Renee pulled back, breaking off the kiss. Inhaling deeply, she reached across her desk and pushed the respond button on her phone. "Yes, Vicki?" she managed to say while heat continued flowing around in her stomach. She glanced over at Tag. The eyes staring at her were smoldering with desire and he was standing there waiting, as if he hadn't finished with her yet.

"Your one-o'clock appointment is here, Ms. Williams."

Renee moistened her lips nervously. Kissing Tag had made her forget everything, including the fact that this was her office and she was standing in the middle of it, kissing him. What if someone had walked in on them? She could imagine the scandal that would have started.

"Thanks, Vicki. Give me a few minutes to wind things up with Mr. Elliott."

Renee then turned her attention back to Tag. He was still standing in the same spot, staring at her. Okay, so she had been the one to initiate the kiss this time. Call them even. It didn't change the fact that they couldn't become involved and she needed to make him understand that. She had more to lose than he did. "A relationship between us won't work, Tag," she said slowly, distinctively stating each word.

"You don't think so?"

"No."

"Because my mother is your patient?"

"Among other reasons that are just as important," she said, deciding to spell it all out for him since he was acting like he didn't have a clue. Surely he could see the obstacles they faced as a couple as well as she could.

He crossed his arms over his chest. "And what are these other reasons?"

"I don't believe in casual affairs, which includes involving myself in relationships that I know upfront won't be going anywhere. You're white and I'm black. You're a wealthy businessman and I'm a social worker whose income won't come close to yours in a million years."

He continued to stare at her. "And your point?"

Renee narrowed her gaze. *Her point?* How could he ask her that when it was so clear? But if he wanted her to break it down even more, then she would. "My point is that I've never dated outside my race. I prefer staying in my comfort zone, and I'm not a woman who ever dreamed of marrying rich."

He laughed, but she could tell he wasn't amused but was rather pissed-off. "Are you saying you're basing your decision on my skin color and my finances?"

Hearing him say it made her feel no better than Thomas Bonner. Immediately, she put her defenses up. "Why would you want to become involved with me, Tag? Come on, let's get real here. Am I a woman your family would expect you to bring to dinner?"

His eyes darkened in anger and he quickly closed the distance between them. "First of all," he said in a low, angry tone, "I don't recall asking you to have a relationship with my family, just with me. Second, my family has never, nor will it ever, dictate how I live my life and with whom. Of course I would be lying if I said I wasn't raised with a certain set of values, but one of the things my grandparents and parents instilled in me more than anything was to judge a person on his character and not his outside appearance. And it's obvious that you're not doing that. If you're judging me by the way I look and by the size of my bank account, then we have nothing left to say."

He turned and walked out the door.

This was one of those days Renee was glad she didn't have any more appointments scheduled after her one o'clock. She needed to leave work as soon as she could to clear her mind of any lingering doubts she had regarding Tag. The words he'd spoken, the accusation, were still hanging there in her mind, refusing to move on. Why had he made things so complicated? Why didn't he understand her decision had been to spare them undue heartache and pain and unnecessary gossip?

Oh, she was sure there were a lot of interracial couples out there falling in love and making things work despite the odds. But it was those odds that bothered her more than anything. He wasn't living on another planet. He knew the rules that society dictated and the problems you could encounter if you decided to go against them.

She remembered all too well Cheryl Hollis and how she had sneaked behind her parents' backs and dated a white guy while they were in high school. Cheryl had gotten pregnant and both set of parents had been up in arms. The guy's parents had money and threatened to cut him off if he so much as claimed the child as his. So he had done exactly as his parents had dictated, leaving Cheryl alone, pregnant and brokenhearted.

Granted, Tag wasn't a high school senior dependent upon his parents' income, but he was still an Elliott. His family's influence and wealth ranked right up there with the Kennedys and Bushes. Heck, his grandmother could probably call Oprah directly and invite her to dinner. Renee ran a frustrating hand down her face. She refused to let Tag lay a guilt trip on her. She wasn't prejudiced, just cautious.

But still, as she shut down her computer for the day, she couldn't erase from her mind that Tag Elliott had done something no other man had been capable of doing since Dionne. He had reminded her she was a woman—a woman with emotions, wants, physical needs and desires. She just wasn't used to a man making her lose control. Even now her palms were sweating just from her thinking about the kiss they had shared earlier here in this office.

She drew in a frustrated breath. No matter what, she had to believe that she had done the right thing letting Tag know where she stood and how she felt. But if that was the case, why was doing the right thing making her feel so bad?

Five

"**I** don't understand what you're saying, Dad. What do you mean Mom doesn't want to see us?" Tag asked, completely baffled.

Michael Elliott met the confused looks of his four offspring. He'd known this conversation would be difficult but somehow he needed to get them to understand how things were with their mother.

"As you know your mother is being released from the hospital today and I'm taking her to The Tides to recuperate. She has requested that when we get there she be left alone for a while. She doesn't want to see anyone. Not even the four of you."

"What?" Tag, Liam, Gannon and Bridget exclaimed simultaneously in shocked voices.

"Are you sure that's what she said, Dad?" Gannon

asked, shaking his head, finding his mother's request hard to believe, totally unacceptable.

Michael nodded sadly. "Yes, and I hope all of you can understand how Karen is feeling right now. She's been through a lot, both emotionally and physically. She needs this time alone."

"What she needs is time with her family," Bridget said, her eyes huge, dark and hurt. "We need to do something if she feels that way. Can't we call her social worker since it's obvious Mom's going through a deep state of depression?"

"I agree with Bridget," Liam said. "There has to be something we can do to lift her spirits."

"I agree as well," Tag chimed in. "I'll visit with Renee Williams to see what can be done." Just saying Renee's name caused pain to ripple through him. It had been almost a week since that day he had angrily walked out of her office. He knew she had visited with his mother a couple of times in the hospital but she'd done so when he hadn't been around to run into her.

"How soon can you meet with Ms. Williams?" Gannon asked, regarding Tag thoughtfully.

"I'll go and see her today."

It was one of those days when Renee had needed to stay at the office after closing hours to get a few things done. She glanced over at the clock as she shut down her computer. It was close to seven o'clock. Normally, she would have left hours ago. Vicki, bless her heart, had hung around to assist Renee in finishing a report.

"I'm out of here," Vicki said smiling, sticking her blond head in the doorway.

Renee returned the older woman's smile. "Thanks for your help. I'm glad we've gotten everything finished for tomorrow's meeting."

"Me, too. I'll see you in the morning. Don't stay too late."

Renee grinned. "Don't worry. I won't be too far behind you."

Minutes later Renee had put everything she needed into her briefcase and glanced up when she heard the knock at the door. Thinking it was the maintenance crew to clean the office, she didn't look up when she said, "Come on in, I'm just about finished and—"

She lifted her head and the rest of the words died on her lips when she saw that the person standing in her doorway was Tag. Suddenly, heat flowed through her body and blood rushed through her veins. He didn't say anything. Neither did she. The silence between them stretched, weaving around them like a silken thread.

Renee breathed in a deep, shuddering breath. She hadn't seen him since that day they'd had words and couldn't help wondering why he was here. They had said everything that could be said and would never see eye to eye on things, so why bother?

Sighing deeply, she closed her briefcase with a click. Instinctively, she squared her shoulders, putting her protection gear in place since it appeared his entire expression was an unreadable mask. But even with that he was a very handsome man. She would always give him that.

"Tag, what are you doing here?"

He stepped into the room and closed the door. "I saw your secretary downstairs and she said you were still here. I need to talk to you."

Renee shook her head. "I don't think there's anything else we need to say."

"I don't want to talk to you about us, Renee. I want to talk to you about my mother." At her raised brow he added, "And that's no lie this time."

It was then that Renee noticed a couple of things about him. His rigid shoulders, the lack of spark in his eyes, the strain of controlled emotions in his features. She quickly crossed the room to him. "What is it, Tag? Has something happened to Karen?"

"No," he said calmly, attempting a faint smile. "Nothing has happened to Mom."

"Then what's wrong?"

He cleared his throat, finding it still hard to believe and even harder to get the words out. "She told Dad that she doesn't want to see any of us while she's recuperating at my grandparents' home."

Renee slowly nodded, understanding. The last time she had met with his mother she could tell that Karen had begun slipping into a state of depression. It had been the same day the doctor had unwrapped her chest to show Karen how to go about caring for her stitches after leaving the hospital, although Renee knew that Michael Elliott had hired a private nurse for his wife.

"None of you should take your mother's request personally, Tag."

Tag's eyebrows snapped together in anger. "What do

you mean we shouldn't take it personally? She's our mother and—"

"She's also a woman with a lot to deal with at the moment. Having both breasts removed isn't something any female would take lightly. For a while, when her chest was bandaged, she was going through denial. But now since she's gotten a chance to see the surgeon's handiwork, reality has set in and she's combating it the only way she knows how, which is with anger, fear and withdrawal. I was with her the day she became angry. Dr. Chaney and I were prepared for it. We were also prepared for the days when she went through stark fear, thinking that perhaps the doctor didn't get all the cancer and it would return to other parts of her body and that she would be eventually lose those parts as well."

Renee sighed deeply, knowing she had to get Tag to accept his mother's present state of mind. Accept it as well as understand it. "Now she's going through withdrawal. She doesn't want to deal with anything or anyone, even those whom she loves. If she could, she would block your father out as well but he won't let her do so, although trust me she has tried."

Tag closed his eyes, not wanting to believe what he was hearing. His mother had always been the strong one in the family. Like his grandmother, she was the one who could always hold things together in a crisis. Now she was going through her own personal crisis and he was finding it hard to conjure up even a little bit of the strength his mother always seemed to have had.

He leaned back against the closed door, suddenly

feeling exhausted. "So what are we supposed to do? Let her continue to wallow in self-pity and do nothing?"

Renee shook her head. "No. To start with, you should all honor her request and give her the space she needs right now, while working together behind the scenes and doing something that can and will lift her spirits."

"Like what?"

Renee shrugged. "Anything that will make her appreciate the fact that she's alive. I understand she enjoys working with her charities. You can arrange for her to continue to do so even while she's convalescing. Remember, she'll be going through both physical and emotional healing. The most important thing is helping her to get beyond her ordeal and concentrate on something else."

Renee studied Tag's expression and knew he had absorbed her words. His next question, however, surprised her. "Will you help, Renee?"

She shook her head. The last thing she needed was complications, and Tag was nothing if not that. "No, I don't think that's—"

"Please."

Renee nervously gnawed the insides of her mouth. Could she handle doing what he was asking? She let out a small breath. Yes, she could handle it if it meant helping Karen. Over the past few weeks she and Tag's mother had developed a relationship that had gone beyond social worker and patient. She admired Karen for all the good things she did for others, especially all her charitable work.

"Will you do it, Renee?"

She glanced into Tag's face and saw the heartfelt

plea in his eyes. And then she knew what her answer would be. "Yes, Tag, I'll help out with your mother any way I can."

Both relief and appreciation shone on his face. "Thank you, Renee. Are you willing to meet with my sister and brothers and explain everything to them as well? Tomorrow night we're having dinner together at Une Nuit, a restaurant owned by my cousin Bryan. Is there any way you can join us there?"

Anyone living in New York had heard of Une Nuit, the restaurant whose patrons oftentimes included a number of celebrities. Now that she had agreed to help him lift Karen's spirits, Renee knew she had to move forward. At least she and Tag wouldn't be dining at the restaurant alone. She wasn't sure how many times she could be alone with him without wanting to comfort him and assure him that everything with his mother would be all right. But she knew to comfort him meant she would also want to kiss him, take his pain away, touch him....

A sexual awareness she only encountered when she was around Tag tried taking over her mind, but she fought it. "Yes, I'll be glad to meet with you and your siblings tomorrow night."

Tag nodded. "I'll pick you up around seven."

"You don't have to do—"

"Yes, I do. I don't want you taking the subway to meet with us. Okay?"

She sighed, knowing his stubbornness was coming out and to argue with him would be pointless. "Fine."

He smiled. "Good. And do you need a ride home now?"

"No, I'm meeting Debbie at a restaurant not far from

here. She's leaving in the morning for an assignment in London so we decided to make it a girls' night out. I'll be fine."

"Are you certain?"

"Yes." She'd never met a man who was so concerned for her well-being. Tag was so thoughtful, caring and attentive.

"Then the least I can do is walk you there."

She knew telling him that wasn't necessary would only be a waste of her time. Clutching her briefcase, she walked out with him, stopping to turn out the lights. Moments later they stepped into the elevator and as the car descended she couldn't help hoping that busybody Diane Carter had left for the day. The last thing Renee needed was to run into her in the lobby. No doubt she'd get the wrong idea about her and Tag.

When the elevator came to a stop and the doors slid open, Tag stood back to let her step out. "You really don't have to walk me to the restaurant, Tag. It's only a few blocks from here," she said, stepping into the hospital lobby. "I'm sure you have more important things to do."

"No," he said, slanting her a sideways glance. "There's nothing more important."

Darkness enfolded them as they stepped outside and began walking. The sidewalks were congested and more than once he gently pulled her closer to him to avoid her getting trampled by someone hurrying past.

When they reached her destination, she turned to him. "Thanks."

"And thank you, Renee, for everything. I'll see you tomorrow night at seven."

"All right."

She quickly entered the restaurant and when she glanced over her shoulder through the window he was still standing there, looking at her.

Tag leaned forward on the conference table with his palms down as he stared at the man and woman sitting at it. "I want anything and everything you can find on Senator Vince Denton, especially his activities over the past year. No one walks away from politics after thirty years without a good reason, especially someone that close to the present administration."

"He gave us his reason. He's been in politics long enough and wants to return to his farm in South Carolina and live the rest of his days in peace and harmony. Sounds like a damn good plan to me," Peter Weston, *Pulse*'s special edition editor, said, carelessly throwing out a paper clip. Peter was responsible for *Pulse*'s campaigns, opinion polls and surveys.

Tag met the man's nonchalant expression. "I don't care how good it sounds, I'm not buying it and I suggest you don't either." He sighed. It was time Tag and his father had a serious talk about Peter's lack of interest in his job. Peter had worked for *Pulse* for over fifteen years, starting out as an investigative reporter—one of the magazine's best—and working his way up through the ranks. Lately, it had been noticed by a number of co-workers that he lacked the hunger, instinct and drive he used to have. Peter had been placed on paid administrative leave on two occasions when his work habits had begun declining and it appeared things were beginning to go downhill again.

Rumor had it that Peter was involved in an affair with a Radio City Rockette and was sacrificing everything, including a good marriage, to be at the woman's beck and call. It was Tag's opinion that what Peter did on his free time was one thing. What he did on *Pulse*'s time was another.

Peter's interest in *Pulse* had started waning a few years ago when Gannon had gotten a position that Peter evidently thought should have been his. He was of the mind that Gannon's name and not his hard work had gotten him where he was, which was not true.

"I thought his resignation was rather strange, too," Marlene Kingston said, scanning the notes she'd taken from an earlier meeting. At twenty-seven, she had been working for *Pulse* since college and always had a good eye for the news. Currently she edited the analysis pages and wrote editorials. "I find it odd that he would resign right before next week's vote on that big oil bill," she added.

Tag liked the woman's sharpness. However, he could tell by the glare Peter had given her that he did not. "That's a good point, Marlene, and one we should look into. Just make sure whatever you have to report is accurate and from a reliable source." He sighed deeply then added, "Pull out all stops and let's dig to see what we can find. Make plans for us to meet in a few days, same time, same place, with some answers."

Half an hour later Tag was poking his head in the room where the smell of ink teased his nostrils. Making his way past old issues of *Charisma*, canisters of ink and reams of paper, not to mention numerous pictures of Elizabeth Taylor plastered on the wall, he made it to the workstation of Edgar Rosewood and sat down in the chair next to it.

The man sitting at the desk looked up at him beneath bushy eyebrows. Edgar, who would be celebrating his seventieth birthday in a few months, had been hired by Patrick within a month of EPH opening its doors, and to this day refused to call it quits by retiring. That was fine with Tag since Edgar had been Tag's father's mentor as well as mentor to Gannon, Liam and himself when they'd come through the ranks. Tag always had and always would consider the man someone special and an asset to *Pulse*. To this day, one thing Edgar retained was a sharp eye for headlines that were so well buried that even a hunting dog couldn't find them.

"What's bothering you, kid?" Edgar asked, his tone rough, his frown deep. "Personal or business?"

Another thing Tag liked about the old man was that he knew how to cut to the chase. Not wanting to delve into his personal problems, not even with Edgar, Tag said, "Business. I think there's more to Senator Denton's resignation than meets the eye."

Edgar swung around from his computer. "So do I."

Tag lifted a paperweight off the pages of last month's magazine. He felt good knowing Edgar was also on to something. "I just hope we can find out what it is before *Time* does."

"We will, as long as you let Marlene Kingston do the digging. She has a nose like a bloodhound. If Denton's not clean, she'll find out just what's dirty. Personally, I like her."

Tag couldn't help but smile. "Why? Because she re-
minds you of a young Elizabeth Taylor?"

The old man smiled. "Yeah, that's one of the reasons.
The other is that she's a good newswoman. The best
thing you can do is get her from under Peter and have
her work with Wayne Barnes. Peter has been taking
credit for Marlene's hard work long enough. The only
interest he seems to have these days is a pair of breasts
pouring out of a Rockette costume. He's doing nothing
but stifling Marlene's growth."

Tag had to agree, which was something else he
needed to talk to Gannon about.

Edgar looked at him, studied him. "You sure there's
nothing else bothering you?"

Tag shrugged. "Of course this thing with Mom is
constantly on my mind."

"That's understandable but I think you might have
another problem."

"What?"

Edgar gave him a pointed look. "The absence of a
good woman in your life."

Tag smiled. Edgar had given him and Liam that
same speech after Gannon had announced his engagement to Erika last month. "Still trying to marry me
off, are you?"

"There's nothing wrong with settling down. I've been
with my Martha for over fifty years and have been involved in a secret love affair with Elizabeth for forty of
those fifty."

Tag chuckled and raised his eyes to the ceiling. "In
your dreams." He stood and checked his watch. A part

of him couldn't wait to see Renee later. He had been thinking about her all day. Gannon, Liam and Bridget were anxious to meet with her tonight as well, to hear what she had to say.

"Time for me to get back to work," Tag said, walking toward the door. He paused in the doorway and stared at the huge poster of Elizabeth Taylor on the wall next to it. "What do you think about when you look at her?" Tag asked Edgar over his shoulder.

He could hear the old man chuckle softly. "Passion and desire."

Tag turned around. "And what do you think about when you look at Martha?"

Edgar stretched out his legs, leaned back in his chair and locked his fingers behind his head. "Same thing, but added to those two is love. And that's the key, kid. Find a woman who can ignite you with passion and desire and who can also fill your heart with love."

Tag grunted. He doubted there was a woman in existence who could fill his heart with love, but when it came to passion and desire there was one face that readily came to mind.

Renee's.

"Thanks for picking me up," Renee said as she eased into the leather seat of Tag's SUV.

"You don't have to thank me, Renee." He closed the door and came around the other side and slid into the driver's seat.

He glanced over at her. "You look nice. But then you always do."

His compliment made her smile. "Thank you."

"You're welcome." He pulled out into traffic.

She was silent, her gaze skimming the buildings and people as they drove by. Although she had never eaten at Une Nuit, she had heard of a lot of nice things about the restaurant. According to what Tag had told her earlier, his cousin Bryan had gotten out of the family business a few years ago to try his hand in the restaurant business. The change in careers had proved successful. Tag had also mentioned that Bryan traveled quite a bit and when he did, the restaurant was managed by a capable Frenchman by the name of Stash Martin.

"My sister and brothers are looking forward to meeting you tonight. They appreciate all you did for our mother while she was in the hospital."

To say what she'd done was merely her job would sound rather cold, Renee thought, especially when she considered the time she'd spent with Karen more valuable than that. She glanced over at Tag. "I'm looking forward to meeting them as well and look forward to doing what I can to help lift your mother's spirits."

When the vehicle came to a stop at a traffic light, she said gently, "Tell me about them." She inhaled sharply when he turned and met her gaze. The depths of his blue eyes shone darkly under a flashing street sign. He did something to her each and every time he looked at her, whether she wanted the reaction or not.

"Gannon, who is thirty-three, is my oldest brother and the second in command to my father at *Pulse*. He always loved his carefree bachelor lifestyle but last month he became engaged to a woman he'd had an affair with over a year ago by the name of Erika Layven. You'll also get to meet her tonight."

Tag hit the brakes when a yellow cab carelessly darted out in front of his Lexus. "Liam," he continued, "is thirty-one and is EPH's financial operating officer." He chuckled. "We tease him about being my grandfather's favorite grandchild because he's the one who keeps tabs on the money, and trust me, he does a damn good job of it. He's sharp when it comes to numbers.

"Last but not least, there's Bridget, who is your age. She's a photo editor for *Charisma* and according to what she tells me, she's still trying to find herself."

He glanced over at Renee. "And there you have it." And with that timely ending, the car came to a stop in front of Une Nuit.

Six

If Renee had felt strange and uncomfortable when she'd first walked into Une Nuit with Tag, then those feelings were definitely behind her now. His siblings had a way of making her feel relaxed, and she could easily tell that the four of them shared a rather close relationship.

The inside of the restaurant looked sensational and the place was filled to capacity, with a number of celebrities in the house. She and Tag bypassed the long line of patrons waiting to be seated and were escorted to the "Elliott Table" where Gannon, Liam and Bridget was waiting for them. Gannon's fiancée, Erika, joined the group a few minutes later.

Tag was quick to explain that with so many family members frequenting the restaurant, Bryan had designated a rear table as the "Elliott Table."

Renee had blinked twice when she'd met the restaurateur. With his jet black hair and blue eyes, she could easily tell that he and Tag were related. And he was so laid-back and friendly.

"Are you sure you don't prefer wine, Renee?" Gannon asked, smiling.

Renee liked Tag's brothers and his sister, as well as Erika. She thought there wasn't a pretentious bone in Erika's body, and like the others, she went out of her way to make her feel comfortable. "No thank you," Renee said. "I better stick with this coffee since there's work tomorrow."

"Yes, there is that. And we want to thank you for your willingness to help with Mom," Gannon said, acting as spokesman for the group. The others nodded in full agreement.

Renee's smile spread to each corner of her lips. "None of you has to thank me. Your mother is a wonderful person and I'm happy to do anything that I can to help her." She had explained earlier exactly what Karen needed. All of them had listened attentively and had thrown out several good ideas and suggestions, but it was Gannon and Erika's suggestion that everyone decided was the best.

In light of Karen's breast cancer, the couple had decided to fly to Vegas and marry at the end of the month instead of having a traditional wedding. However, if planning a wedding would give Karen something to do and lift her spirits, they would certainly change their plans. It was decided that Erika would contact Karen and ask her assistance in planning a small wedding.

The family had already made plans to gather at Patrick and Maeve's Hampton estate at the end of the month to celebrate the older couple's anniversary, and Gannon and Erika thought it would be special to exchange their vows on the same exact date Gannon's grandparents had fifty-seven years ago. Since everyone knew how much Karen loved planning special events, they hoped assisting Erika with her wedding would lift Karen's spirits.

While Renee sipped her coffee she couldn't help but notice when Gannon leaned over to Erika and whispered something into her ear. Whatever he said brought a smile to Erika's face, and she tilted her head for him to kiss her on the lips. Renee was touched by the romantic gesture, just one of several that had passed between the couple that night. She'd been surprised by how open they had been in admitting their love for each other and their desire to get married and start a family right away.

"Ready to leave?"

Renee nearly jumped when Tag leaned over and whispered into her ear. She lifted her gaze but she didn't dare move her head. Doing so would have their lips practically touching. Yet, they were so close there was no way their breath wouldn't mingle when she did speak. "Yes, I'm ready."

She regretted having to say good-night to everyone and was surprised when Bridget slipped her business card into her hand and told her to call her one day soon so the two of them could do lunch. Erika did the same thing.

"I enjoyed myself tonight," Renee said to Tag when they were in the SUV and on their way back to her place. "You have special siblings, and after meeting your parents I can see why. They did a great job in raising all of you."

Tag glanced over at her and smiled. "Thanks." Although she had given him a compliment, he couldn't forget it had just been a few days since she had stood in her office and practically said she could not have a relationship with him because of their different races and his family's wealth.

"What's this joke about the family feud?"

Renee's question interrupted Tag's thoughts. He glanced over at her. "It's no joke, it's the truth. My grandfather is retiring at the end of the year and has decreed that whoever makes their magazine the biggest success by the end of the year will be given the position of CEO of EPH."

Renee glanced at him with widened eyes. "You're kidding, right?"

Tag chuckled. "No, I wish I was but I'm dead serious. And what's so crazy is that although the four magazines are run by a different offspring, the staff is mixed. For example, Bridget doesn't work with me, Gannon and my father at *Pulse*. She works with Aunt Finola at *Charisma*. So in essence, in trying to put *Charisma* on top, she won't be rallying to our father's side in his bid for the CEO position."

"Uh-oh, that can be a pretty sticky position to be placed in," Renee said, wondering why Tag's grandfather would do such a thing in pitting his family against each other that way.

"It already is and personally, I don't like it. The feud

between the different magazines is making things tense at the office."

Renee turned her head and recognized the deli on the corner. They were within a block of her place. She shifted in her seat, suddenly feeling nervous. When Tag had picked her up earlier she had been dressed and ready to go and had walked out of the apartment before he'd had a chance to knock. She couldn't help wondering, considering their argument in her office over a week ago, if he would just drop her off at the curb and keep going. She had to be realistic enough to know that the only reason he had shown up at her office last night was to ask for her help with his mother.

When his car turned the corner and came to a stop in front of her apartment building, she began unbuckling her seat belt. In a way, she was sorry the ride had ended. "Thanks again for tonight."

"I should be thanking you, and I do," he said huskily, seconds before opening his door and quickly walking in front of the car to open the car door for her. He offered her his hand.

She took it and immediately felt flushed from the top of her head all the way to her toes. All it took was a look in his eyes to know he'd felt it, too. Tingles of awareness were electrifying the space between them. A yearning sensation was spreading all through her limbs and she suddenly longed for the feel of his lips on hers. She blinked, forcing those thoughts away, and knew she had to take control of what was happening to her. Put a stop to it immediately.

They didn't say anything as he walked her to her

apartment, and when they reached her door he stood silently by while she took the key from her purse and unlocked it. She turned to him. "Thanks for walking me to the door, Tag."

"You don't have to thank me, Renee."

If she had been focused more on her surroundings than on Tag, Renee would not have noticed the deep timbre of his voice or the intensity that filled his blue eyes. But she did notice those things although she wished she hadn't, because in doing so she felt more heat spread through her.

She remembered their conversation that day in her office. She knew every single word she had told him, could probably recite it in her sleep. But now, at this very moment, none of it mattered. She was dealing with an emotion she'd never dealt with before and she knew, whether she wanted it to happen or not, she had fallen in love with Tag.

Forbidden love.

She sucked in a deep breath at the realization and wondered how she could have let such a thing happen. The big question was not how he had gotten through her defenses so quickly, but how he had managed to get through them at all. They were completely wrong for each other, on different ends of a spectrum, worlds apart. They could never share a happy life together without stares and frowns. There was no reason to think about a future with him, but there was something they could share tonight that would be theirs and theirs alone.

"Good-night, Renee." Tag leaned down and kissed her cheek before turning to leave. He took a few steps, stopped, and then, as if he was compelled to look at her just one more time, he turned back around.

The moment their gazes reconnected she knew she was doomed. She loved him and she wanted him. It was as simple as that. At least for tonight it would be simple. "Would you like to come in for a drink or something?" she asked softly, unable to hold her silence any longer.

With a smile that would have endeared him to her for life if he hadn't already been so, he recovered the distance separating them and whispered, "Are you sure you want to be alone with me tonight, Renee?"

Emotions clogged her throat. She knew what he was asking.

He had tried walking away but couldn't. Like her, he had reached the end of his rope. Desire had thickened their minds, taken control of their thoughts, and, God forbid, pushed them over the edge. Once they stepped into her apartment there would be no turning back and they both knew it.

"Yes, I'm sure," she said, her mind completely made up. They would have this night together. With that decision made, an unexpected rush of relief and pleasure washed over her, forcing any and all opposition from her mind. He was man. She was woman. And at this moment, he was the man she loved and wanted.

"If you're sure," he said, slowly opening the door.

"And I am," she said as an assured smile touched the corners of her lips.

"In that case, I think we should take this inside."

He held the door open to let her go in first and then he followed, closing and locking the door behind him.

* * *

There was definitely something sexual and elemental about being alone with the woman you desperately wanted, Tag thought as he leaned against the closed door.

He watched as Renee went to stand in the middle of the room. She was nervous. He could tell. But then he was aroused and he knew that she could tell that as well. There was no way his body could keep something like that a secret. He suddenly felt like holding her in his embrace, needing to feel the heat of her body against his.

He held his hand out to her. "Come here, Renee," he said in a voice that wanted to retain control but was slowly losing it.

She placed her purse on a table and crossed the room to stand in front of him. His hands automatically slid around her waist. "I want to hold you for a little while," he said, bringing her body closer to the fit of him. Renee's head automatically rested upon his chest.

Tag knew there were still unresolved issues between them but at this very moment, while she was in his arms, nothing mattered but them being together this way. What was important was that when it came to passion and desire they were in accord.

Passion and desire.

Edgar's words rang loudly in Tag's ears. He thought of all the other women he'd ever dated, some as stunning as a woman could get, but there was something about Renee that was different. She was as beautiful as the rest but there was this ingrained, unadulterated sense of kindness and decency that pulled him to her each and every time.

"Tag?" she whispered moments later, the warmth of her breath splaying against his cheek.

"Mmm?"

"Are we going to stand here like this all night?"

His lips parted in a smile. Only Renee could ask such a question at a time like this. Instead of answering her, he bent and swept her into his arms at the exact moment his mouth settled hungrily over hers. It was by no means a gentle kiss and was intended to let her know just how much he desired her.

She moaned and the sound intensified the deep-rooted longing within him. He pulled his mouth away briefly to ask, "Which way to the bedroom?"

"Down the hall then to your right."

Holding her tight against him, he moved in that direction. When they reached the bedroom doorway he resumed kissing her, letting his tongue explore and devour every inch of her mouth. Somehow, with their lips locked, they made it to the bed. He was grateful she had left a lamp on in the room.

She gave a nervous laugh and pulled him down on the soft mattress with her. He tilted his head back and looked at her, thinking that he'd never wanted a woman as much as he wanted Renee. Anticipation filled his entire being as he slipped off the bed to remove his clothes.

He watched her watch him remove his shirt then he reached his hand out and pulled her off the bed to him. After removing her shoes he turned her around to work at the zipper on her dress. He liked her dress, a silky-looking A-line blue dress that showed off her shapely figure. He had definitely liked seeing her in it, but would enjoy seeing her out of it even more.

"I've wanted you from that first day I walked into your office," he whispered, placing a wet kiss on her shoulder. He felt a shudder race through her body and gloried in the fact that he had been the one to make it happen.

"You did?"

"Yes, and it shook me up some because I've never wanted a woman that much before."

He slid the zipper down and then pushed the garment off her shoulders. All it took was for Renee to do one sensuous shimmy of her hips and the dress fell in a heap at her feet. Next, on one bended knee, he removed her panty hose, leaving her clad in the sexiest bra and panty set he'd ever seen. Simply seeing the baby-blue lace against her dark skin made his loins tighten. Added to that were her gorgeous legs and bright red painted toenails that matched the color of her fingernails. He was of the opinion that for all intents and purposes, she took the word *sexy* to a whole new level. She was the epitome of every male fantasy, definitely his own. His mind began spinning, blood pumped hot and heavy through his veins as he unbuckled his belt and began removing his pants.

From their first kiss he had been fighting the need to make love to her. She was constantly in his thoughts, even when he hadn't wanted her there. Fantasizing about her had become his favorite pastime.

He tossed his pants aside and stood before her wearing only his briefs, and suddenly felt a jolt of desire when she reached out and slid her hand down his chest, letting her fingers slowly work their way beneath the waistband of his underwear to curl around his rock-hard erection. And when she began stroking him, he thought he was going to lose it. He *knew* he was going to lose it if she didn't stop.

"Renee…"

"Yes?"

Her response was as innocent as it could get and he quickly decided that two could definitely play her game. And in this case, two definitely would. He sat down on the edge of the bed and gently pulled her to him to straddle his hips. His hands spanned her waist just before they began kneading her buttocks. He liked the feel of her soft skin and the scent of her as well. Damn, she smelled good.

And when she leaned forward and began nuzzling his jaw with her lips and running her hands over his shoulder and chest, he inhaled sharply, gripping her hips and pushing upward, wanting her to feel just what she was doing to him, how deeply aroused he was.

His mouth captured hers as he lay back, bringing her atop him in the process, the softness of her flesh sinking into him. Moments later she lifted her mouth and stared down at him. "We still have some clothes on," she whispered in the silence of the room.

He shifted his body, placed her beneath him and then leaned up and began removing her bra. The moment he uncovered her breasts, his senses jolted and desire slammed into him. They were high, sensuously shaped with protruding dark-tipped nipples that seemed to beg for his tongue. There was no way he could resist.

He cupped a breast in his hand as his mouth greedily latched onto it and began devouring it with deep male appreciation and far-reaching primitive hunger, trying to pull all the sweetness out of it. A rapturous gasp tore from deep within her throat, and moments later, when she shuddered and cried out his name, he was amazed that she had climaxed just from him kissing her breasts.

Good. It would make what he intended to do next even more enjoyable for the both of them. He pulled back slightly, ran his hands down her thighs, fingering the edge of her lace panties. He touched her there in the center and found the fabric damp. He was definitely grateful for that.

Without wasting any time, he removed her panties and then just as quickly he leaned back and removed his own underwear. He looked at her and immediately thought of a chocolate sundae, his favorite treat. He leaned forward and began nuzzling the soft skin of her flat stomach, licking the area around her navel. Her feminine scent surrounded him, making his body harden even more.

"Tag, what are you doing?" she asked, barely able to get the words out.

He lifted his mouth long enough to say, "I'm about to eat you alive, sweetheart. You look beautiful, sexy and delicious." As soon as those words left his mouth he eased his head between her open legs and captured her with his mouth, kissing her there.

"Tag!"

He didn't let up and when she began squirming beneath his mouth, he gripped her hips to keep her still as his tongue continued to devour her in this very intimate way. The succulent taste of her pushed him over the edge and made him even greedier, as desire rocketed through his veins, making him growl low in his throat.

He felt her feminine muscles suddenly clench beneath his mouth and then she came and his tongue savored each and every orgasmic vibration that filled him with more of her taste. She rocked her pelvis upward at the same time as she screamed out his name again.

Before she could catch her next breath, he quickly put on a condom and then eased his body over hers, positioning his erection right smack against her satiny flesh, settling his hips in the cradle between her thighs.

"Open your eyes and look at me, Renee."

Their eyes met and the glaze of stark passion he saw there filled him with male satisfaction. "Don't see color when you look at me," he whispered huskily as he began easing inside of her. "Don't think of social status when you feel me inside of you," he continued, his voice rough and low. "Think of passion, desire. Think of me…the man who wants you."

He continued going deeper into her, holding her gaze. "Say my name, baby."

Renee bit her lip, trying to stop the fears of the future from overtaking her mind. She knew if she said his name now, when they were like this, it would become embedded in her soul forever. He had already found a way into her heart, but to take part of her soul…

"Say it."

Tag tilted his head up and stared down at her. He was

buried deeply inside of her, to the hilt. He hadn't wanted to hurt her but she had been so tight and entering her hadn't been easy. He held still, refusing to move his hips until she acknowledged that what they were sharing was passion between a man and a woman, and color and social status had nothing to do with it. On this point he was determined to be of one accord with her. In a voice that was lower still, he whispered, "Speak my name."

Renee dug her fingers into his back, unable to fight it any longer. He was so intensely male that she knew who he was and what he was to her, whether she wanted to admit it or not. She would admit it but on her own terms. "Speak mine," she countered.

He stared at her and smiled and brushed his fingertips against her cheek. "Renee," he said huskily.

The caress was so tender that she fell deeper in love with him at that precise moment. "Tag." And as every cell in her body vibrated in response to his touch, she said his name again. "Tag."

He leaned down and buried his face in the curve of her neck, holding her close to him. Now that they had put things into prospective, at least for the time being, Tag began moving inside of her, mating with her in a way he'd never done with another woman. He felt the quivering deep in her womb with each and every push and pull. He feasted on her mouth, on her breasts while he increased the pressure, multiplied the thrusts and enhanced their bodies' rhythm.

Moments later when she flew apart, he was flying right along with her. A release, of a magnitude he had never before experienced, ripped from him, shattering him to a degree that made his thighs quake. The low, guttural sound from his throat was necessary to keep the veins from popping in his neck when he threw his head back. He was worshipping her body, claiming her as his.

And he knew when another climax suddenly rammed through him, to piggyback with the first, that no matter what protests Renee might continue to make about them pursuing a relationship, there was no way he could ever let her go.

"I don't want to leave you tonight," Tag's dark-velvet voice murmured softly against Renee's ear, bringing her awake.

She opened her eyes and gazed up into his deep-blue ones and gave him a sleepy smile as she thought of all they had done together for the past few hours. "Then don't."

"Is that an invitation?" he asked, leaning down and kissing her jaw, savoring the line around her lips with his tongue.

Renee's senses immediately responded. "Yes," she purred against his lips. "That's an invitation."

She wrapped her arms around his neck and parted her mouth to welcome his strong, hot tongue that started seducing her all over again, sucking her very breath. At the same time his hand traveled down her naked body to the apex of her thighs. Within minutes he had her writhing and moaning into his mouth.

He slowly lifted his lips from hers and his gaze roamed over her face as he pulled a shuddering breath into his lungs. "I can't get enough of you, Renee. It's like you're entrenched within every pore in my body."

She watched as he stood to pull another condom from his wallet and swiftly roll it into place. When he returned to the bed she held his gaze as he slid his body over hers once more, her thighs automatically opening for him. Like dry tinder, her body ignited when joined to his, and she could feel the tension building inside of her as she raced forward, fast and furious, toward the release he was driving her to.

Moments later she screamed his name, as she felt herself shattering into a thousand pieces. He continued his intimate strokes, withholding his release with iron-clad control while pushing deeper and deeper still. Ecstasy seized her once again and a sensuous cry tore from her lips at the same time she felt him buck and call out her name.

Tag continued to murmur her name repeatedly and it sounded like music to her ears. She slid her hands up over the tense muscles of his back, kneading them as she savored the slow aftermath of what they were sharing. A part of her knew it was time to start pulling back. She was falling in love with him even more and was beginning to need him too desperately.

She knew if she didn't start thinking straight that she would find herself in deep trouble, but at that moment the only thing she wanted to think about was Teagan Elliott, what he meant to her and how he was making her feel.

Seven

Tag slowly began waking just as the first light of morning shone into the room. He breathed in deeply as Renee's sensuous, womanly scent was drawn into his nostrils.

Shifting his body, he glanced over at the empty spot in the bed but relaxed at the sound of the shower. He looked at the clock. It was a little past six. He sprawled on his back and threw one arm across his face to ward off the daylight that was coming through the window blinds. Instinctively, he ran a tongue over his top lip and discovered the taste of Renee was still there, and without any control he released a groan of pleasure at the memory.

Last night had been special to him in many ways and even now his body was exhausted, drained from spent passion. But if she were to walk out of the bathroom, he would be revived and want her all over again.

But by no means, regardless of how sexually compatible they were, did he think what they were sharing was all about sex and nothing more. He had been there with other women, but this thing with Renee was different. He sighed as an unexplainable sensation began developing deep within his chest and a breath he hadn't realized he'd been holding forced its way from his lungs. He wasn't sure what any of this meant but he did know that no matter what problems she thought they had, they would work them out because he had never wanted a woman like he wanted Renee.

With that thought in mind he shifted back on his stomach, buried his head into the pillow and slowly drifted off to sleep again.

Renee adjusted the shower cap on her head as she stood beneath the spray of water. The soreness in her thighs and the area between her legs were a blatant reminder of how long it had been since she had made love to a man, and never with the intensity of what she had shared with Tag.

She had lost count of the number of times they had come together during the night, but each time the pleasure had intensified even more. She had slept with only two other men in her lifetime, a guy she'd dated in college and Dionne. Neither had had the time or the inclination to prolong their lovemaking, and would never have considered withholding their own pleasure to make sure that she soared to the highest peak.

But Tag had.

He had proven there wasn't a selfish bone in his body when it had come to pleasuring her, and no woman could ask for more than that. The thought of everything he'd done made her quiver, deep down in her womb.

She sighed deeply. It was a new day and with it came all the insecurities of yesterday. Nothing had changed. He was white and she was black; he was rich and she was a working girl. But none of that could stop her from thinking about how right he had looked in her bed when she'd slipped out of it, being careful not to wake him. Although it was Friday, it was a busy workday for her, but Tag had a position within his family's company where he could make his own hours, and since he hadn't gotten much sleep last night, there was no telling when he would wake up.

Turning off the water, she stepped out of the shower. She had meetings most of the day and couldn't afford to be late. She would be as quiet as she could while dressing for work. She wasn't used to having a houseguest, especially one like Tag.

Tag awoke with a jolt at the sound of a car backfiring. He sat up and glanced at the empty spot in the bed beside him and saw the note pinned to the pillow.

I had to leave for work. Thanks for everything last night. Renee.

A smile touched his lips. She was always thanking him whether he wanted her to or not. But in this case it should be him thanking her. Everything they had shared had been special and he had gotten the best sleep he had in a long time, ever since that outrageous feud between the magazines and his mother's bout with cancer.

Last night he and Renee had shared a night of passion but he wondered what her thoughts were today. Would she allow their relationship to move to the next level without making a big deal out of things? Maybe it was pure possessiveness on his part, but he didn't intend to wait around for her to call the shots. He wanted to be with her, to continue to share this special relationship with her and he refused to let her end things between them before they got started. Somehow he had to show her that with them, color and social status didn't matter. And he intended to start doing so today.

Getting out of bed, he crossed the room to dig his cell phone out of his pants pocket. Within minutes he had his secretary on the line. "Joanne, clear my calendar of any appointments and meetings this morning. I won't be coming in before noon. And tell Gannon to call me the minute he gets back from his meeting with Rick Howard."

He then placed a call to his father to check on his mother. The news wasn't too uplifting. His mother was still withdrawn, not very talkative and still wasn't ready to see her children.

Sighing deeply, he then placed a call to a florist and ordered a dozen red roses to be delivered to Renee. And last but not least, he dialed the phone number for his good friend Alton Malone.

"Hey, Al, this is Tag. That painting you had displayed at Hollis on Saturday, I want it."

He smiled when his friend joked about Tag having enough of his paintings already. "It's not for me but for someone I've met. Someone special."

Tag laughed when he heard Alton pretend to be gasping for breath. Like Tag's siblings, Alton knew how limited his time was when it came to indulging in affairs. "Okay, knock it off, and yes, I think she's special. I think she's very special."

Renee leaned back in her chair and stared at the vase of flowers that had arrived that day. To say they were beautiful would be an understatement, and it didn't take long for word to get around the office that Renee Williams, the quiet, keeps-to-herself social worker who never dated, must have finally found a boyfriend since she had gotten flowers—and a dozen long-stem red roses at that.

She was glad she had taken off the card and inserted it into her desk drawer before Diane had breezed into her office to see the flowers that everyone was whispering about. Diane had looked high and low for the card, evidently feeling she had every right to read it.

But as far as Renee was concerned, it was a card meant for her to read in private, and since she had a few moments alone now, she pulled it out of her desk and reread Tag's words.

Last night meant more to me than you'll ever know. Have dinner with me tonight so I can thank you properly. Tag.

Renee sighed. According to Vicki, Tag had called twice while she had been in meetings. More than likely he wanted to confirm that she would be free to go out to dinner with him tonight.

She stood and went to the window. Although there was no way she would regret what she shared with Tag last night, a part of her knew it may have sent him the wrong message. Her thoughts and feelings on them dating hadn't changed. She wished things could be different but they weren't and she had accepted that. If only he would.

She turned when the phone rang on her desk and quickly crossed the room to pick it up. "Yes, Vicki?"

"Mr. Teagan Elliott is on the line for you."

Renee briefly closed her eyes, inhaled deeply. "All right, please put him through." Her legs felt weak as she eased into the chair behind her desk.

"Renee."

She swallowed upon hearing the sound of her name from Tag's lips, those same lips he had used to make love to her. His skill and virility in the bedroom surpassed anything she'd ever known. "Yes, Tag, it's Renee."

"How are you feeling?"

She knew why he was asking. No woman made love as many times as they had last night without feeling some discomfort. But then a part of her didn't mind the discomfort. The pleasure she had received had made any discomfort well worth it. "I'm feeling okay, and you?"

"I feel better than I've felt in a long time and you're the reason."

She nervously licked her lips as she glanced across

the room at the flowers. "Thanks for the roses. They're beautiful."

"And so are you. I don't think there's an inch on your body that isn't beautiful."

Abruptly she flushed and moved her gaze away from the flowers, remembering just how much of her body he had seen, touched, tasted. Red-hot embers swiftly flickered to life within her, forcing her to remember every moment, every intimate detail. "Tag, I don't think…" Her voice trailed off. The fact of the matter was that at the moment she couldn't think. She could only remember, and the memories were overwhelming her.

"Have dinner with me tonight, Renee. I want to take you someplace special."

She leaned back in the chair and closed her eyes. "Tag, I don't think that's a good idea."

"And I happen to think it's a wonderful idea, unless…"

Involuntarily, she reopened her eyes. "Unless what?"

"Unless you're ashamed to be seen with me."

She sat straight up in her chair. "That's not it and you know it," she defended stubbornly. "I have been seen with you. I was with you last Saturday and again last night."

"But I don't consider those real dates. I want to take you out to dinner and dancing."

"But I've told you that I don't think it's a good idea for us to take things further," she implored, desperately needing for him to understand. Why couldn't he get it that they were from two different worlds in more ways than one?

"Too late, sweetheart. We've already taken things

further. In my book they can't get any further then they got last night. You might chalk it up to merely a night of passion, a night we lost our heads to lust, but I consider it something more solid and substantial. If you don't think so, then I need to convince you otherwise. Don't try to make what we shared last night nothing more than casual and fun. It *was* more and you know it."

Renee bowed her head. Yes, she knew it. She also knew something else that he didn't know. She loved him.

"Have dinner with me tonight, Renee. Please."

Renee lifted her head. What would it hurt if she had dinner with him? Maybe she could use that time to convince him there were too many issues facing them in a relationship. And then there was the fact that she did want to be with him, share time with him, make love to him again, even though she shouldn't.

"All right. I'll have dinner with you."

"Great! I'll make reservations on board the Harbor."

Renee swallowed. The Harbor wasn't just any dinner cruise ship. It was one that sailed down the Hudson River while catering to the affluent. She'd heard that you had to be a member of the private club to even step on deck, and that the prices were so high she'd never go there in her lifetime and definitely not on her budget. "The Harbor? It's still running, even in February?"

"As long as the weather cooperates, it sails. And I'd like you and I to be on it. What do you say?"

Renee exhaled. How could she possibly tell him no? "Okay."

"And I'll pick you up around seven. Is that time all right?"

"Yes, seven is fine."

"Good. I'll see you then."

Moments after hanging up the phone, Renee couldn't help wondering if she had gotten in deeper than she should have. After all, the deeper she got, the harder it would be to eventually walk away.

Tag glanced first at Gannon then back at Marlene Kingston, not knowing exactly what to say. He'd had a hunch that Senator Denton's resignation hadn't been as benign as it seemed. "And you're sure about this, Marlene? Can we trust our sources?" Tag was well aware how the use of anonymous sources by news organizations had been under heightened scrutiny over the past year.

"Yes, more than you can guess. Here's the name," she said, handing him a sheet of paper.

Tag took the paper and glanced at it, then raised a brow before passing it on to Gannon. After reading it, Gannon whistled. The name on the paper was that of the senator's niece. "This is definitely a strictly confidential source. How did you manage it?"

Marlene smiled. "Jeanette and I attended classes together at Georgetown. Once I started asking questions she broke down and told me everything. She's a highly ethical person and over the years found anomalies in the Senator's behavior that she didn't approve of. She's always felt compelled to keep quiet, but this last thing was the final straw. As you can see, we have a reliable story here, Tag. And what's even more special is that it seems *Time* doesn't even have a clue, which gives us an advantage."

Tag sighed. Marlene's source indicated that Senator Denton had participated in a cover-up in the worse possible way and it was up to *Pulse* to report it. Not only did the American people have a right to know but Tag knew what being the first to print the article would do for sales. It would definitely put *Pulse* ahead in his grandfather's competition game. Big headlines brought in readers, and readers drove the profits up.

Gannon stood and rubbed a hand down his face. "We're going to have to have all our ducks in a row for this one. Senator Denton is well-liked and highly respected, and a cover-up of this magnitude will cause one hell of a scandal. But I want *Pulse* to be the one to expose it."

Tag smiled, feeling the adrenaline rush he'd always experienced when they were on the verge of breaking a story. Top that off with his dinner date tonight with Renee and he felt like a man riding high above the clouds.

"I'll finalize my report and have it on Peter's desk by Monday," Marlene said, interrupting his thoughts.

Tag shook his head. "No. This is going to be your story. You're doing all the digging and the Senator's niece is your contact. You write the article."

Gannon nodded in agreement. "Where the hell is Peter, anyway?"

"He's still at lunch," Marlene said, gathering up all her papers to put in her briefcase.

After Marlene had left, Tag looked over at Gannon and said, "We're going to have to do something about Peter. He knew about this meeting."

Gannon was about to respond when the phone on his desk rang. He quickly picked it up when he saw it was his private line. Tag, who figured the caller was probably Erika and didn't want to intrude on his brother's private conversation, strolled across the room to look out the window. It was a beautiful day, and seeing all the red paper hearts being displayed in the store window across the street reminded him that Tuesday was Valentine's Day.

"That was Dad."

Tag turned and met his brother's smiling face. Evidently their father had called with good news. "And?"

Gannon grinned. "He called to say that Erika talked to Mom and she agreed to help out with the wedding." Gannon's smile widened even more when he added, "Dad also wanted me to tell you, Liam and Bridget that Mom wants to see us on Sunday for dinner."

A smile broke on Tag's face. Although Renee had explained to him what his mother was going through, it hadn't been easy to be shut out by her. "Hey, that's great!"

Gannon chuckled. "Yes, it is, and we have Renee to thank for helping us come up with a plan to boost Mom's spirit. Thank her when you see her again."

Tag lifted a curious brow. "And what makes you think I'll see her again?"

Gannon met Tag's stare and grinned. "You will. I saw the way you were looking at her at dinner the other night. You are definitely interested in her. I like her and you're right, she's beautiful."

Tag absently picked up a paper clip on his brother's desk and said, "I'm taking her out tonight. To the Harbor." He was excited about his and Renee's official date and didn't mind sharing it with his brother.

Gannon raised a brow as he leaned back in his chair. "The Harbor? So, I'm right in assuming you're interested in her."

Tag moved toward the door and slid his brother a parting glance. "Yes, I'm definitely interested."

From where Renee was standing at her bedroom window she could see a silver-gray Mercedes sports car stop in front of her apartment building. The way her heart began beating she knew it was a different vehicle but the same man.

Tag.

She couldn't help standing there, watching as he exited from the vehicle. He said he would be by to pick her up at seven but for some reason she'd known he would arrive a few minutes early.

She couldn't help but study him as he made his way to her apartment door, his stride long, his steps hurried, unusual for a man who wasn't late getting to where he was going. He wore a black suit and even from where Renee stood she could tell it was made from the highest quality fabric and probably had a designer name attached to it. Tag had Hollywood good looks and watching him was forcing her to participate in one hell of a mind exercise.

Suddenly, as if sensing that he was being watched, Tag glanced up and their eyes connected and Renee felt it, just as surely as if he had been able to defy logic and actually reach up and touch her. He smiled and goose bumps began to rise on her arms, her heart literally skipped a beat, and when he waved up at her, she couldn't do anything but lift her hand and wave back. Turning away from the window, she braced herself for the man who was doing a good job of rocking her world.

Moments later she stood in front of the door, her stomach knotting, her breasts becoming sensitive, a tender ache in certain muscles. Forcing herself to get a grip, she opened the door.

Whatever Renee had expected, it hadn't been Tag sweeping her into his arms and closing the door behind him with the heel of his shoe and then hungrily capturing her mouth, locking it with his as if joining them with some kind of magnetic force, immediately driving her mad with desire. She wrapped her arms around him and whimpered, the sound quickly drowned out by their heavy breathing.

Renee quickly came to the conclusion that she could go without dinner if she could remain here and feast on Tag. When he finally released her mouth and placed her back on her feet, she pressed her face into his chest, thinking that no one had ever kissed her hello quite that way before.

She looked up at him when she felt his hand glide through her hair, and then he was lifting her chin up and leaning down for yet another kiss. There was no way she could not respond to this. To him. Whether she wanted it to or not, loving him was taking her beyond any boundaries she wanted to set. When it came to Tag there were no limitations, but she had a feeling there was unchartered territory that he planned for them to explore. Together.

"I thought of you a lot today," he said, his voice

strained. As he whispered against her ear, his tongue flicked out to taste her skin there.

"And I thought of you a lot today, too," she replied honestly. She hated herself for admitting such a thing but knew she had to admit it anyway.

Slowly, he took a step back and looked at her and then he captured her hand in his, held it above her head and twirled her around, letting the ruffles at the hem of her black dress swirl about her ankles. "You look gorgeous tonight, Renee."

She knew he meant every word and was glad that she had left the office early to do a little shopping. "Thanks."

He took a step closer to her and leaned down and kissed her slowly, thoroughly. Moments later, Renee slipped from his arms. "If we don't leave now we might be late," she said, her pulse racing fast and furiously.

Tag smiled. "You're right. But then I'll have something to look forward to after dinner, won't I?"

Renee swallowed as she nodded. She would have something to look forward to after dinner as well.

The Harbor was a beautiful dinner cruise ship and the moment they stepped on deck via a heated tented walkway, a uniformed waiter escorted them to their table in the Tropicana Room.

Renee glanced around, tempted to pinch herself. This was a new ship and everything looked elegant and expensive, including the marble floors and crown molding. Tag squeezed her hand and smiled down at her. "I hope you like the setting."

She gave him an assuring grin. "Trust me, I do."

They were shown to a white-linen-covered table with a huge glass window that provided a panoramic view of the Hudson. After handing them menus, the waiter left them alone just as the ship began moving. Soft music was playing and not far away a dance floor was set up for dancing later. Muted conversation filled the rooms as hosts and hostesses escorted other arrivals to their tables.

Renee had never been on a cruise before and when she felt the movement of the ship she planted her feet firmly on the floor. "I can't believe we're actually moving," she said nervously.

Tag chuckled. "We are. We'll be out on the Hudson for a couple of hours or so."

She nodded. "You come here often?"

He smiled at her. "I've dined here a number of times with various members of my family." And then, because he wanted her to know just how special tonight was to him, Tag added, "But this is the first time I've ever brought a date here."

Renee opened her mouth, then immediately closed it when nothing came out. The thought that she was the first made her entire body tingle in appreciation, blatantly ignoring the warning signs of what doing so could mean. "Thank you," she said politely.

His smile widened. "You're always thanking me."

"Because you're always doing something nice."

He leaned forward in his chair and whispered, "Can't help it with you. You bring out the best in me."

"And I'm supposed to believe that?" she asked, chuckling.

"I hope you do because it's the truth."

At that moment the waiter returned with a bottle of wine. "I asked for a bottle to be brought out before our meal so we can toast my good news," Tag told her.

Renee lifted a brow. "And what good news is that?" She could tell he'd been in a rather good mood but he hadn't shared the reason for it her during the car ride from her apartment. Instead he had told her how his day had gone at work and she shared tidbits about hers.

"Good news about Mom. Dad called to tell us that she has agreed to help Erika with her wedding and that she also wants to see all of us on Sunday for dinner."

Renee's face beamed with happiness. She knew how much his mother's depression had bothered Tag. "Oh, Tag, that's wonderful! It will take her concentration off her condition and put it on something else. I told you that planning Erika's wedding would do wonders for her."

"Yes, you did tell us, didn't you? And Gannon asked me to thank you for all the advice you gave to us last night. We will be forever in your debt."

For some reason the thought of Tag thinking he owed her something didn't sit well with Renee. "Neither you nor your family owes me anything, Tag. Like I told all of you that night, I like your mother, I think she's a special person and I empathized with all of you. I just wanted to help."

That was exactly what he found so special about Renee. She had such a sweet spirit about her and a passionate spirit as well, judging from last night. The memory of them coming apart in each other's arms was etched deep into his brain.

He had a lot going on in his life with his mother and work, but he couldn't imagine not carving out this time to spend with Renee. "Let's make a toast," he said, lifting his glass. "To my mother's continued good health."

Renee held up her glass to his. "Yes, to Karen's continued good health."

Renee thought that everything about tonight was perfect. The man, the cruise down the Hudson River and the cozy atmosphere. Over dinner they talked more about his mother, his grandfather's outlandish proposal and he provided tidbits on his other family members, especially all the cousins he was close to. It was the information on his grandfather that intrigued her the most.

"Things will work out, Tag, I'm sure of it. From everything you've told me, family means a lot to your grandfather. I can't imagine him doing anything to intentionally destroy that. There must be a reason for what you and your family see as his madness. I've discovered in life that things aren't always as they seem to be."

Tag wondered if she felt that way about them. He clearly remembered what she'd told him that day in her office. Still, she had agreed to go out with him tonight, and he hoped that last night meant as much to her as it did to him. Was she willing for them to give things a try? He was convinced they should continue to see each other, but knew convincing her of that wouldn't be easy. But he would not give up.

"Would you like dessert?" he asked, after the waiter had returned to clear their table. The river was beautiful and the cruise was setting the mood for romance. During several lulls in their conversation, heat and desire had surrounded them. He had felt it and knew that she had felt it, too.

Renee smiled. "No. I doubt that I could eat a single thing more. Everything was delicious, Tag. Thanks for bringing me here."

"It was my pleasure. Would you like to dance?"

Renee heard the soft, slow music and had been noticing several couples move on the dance floor during different times all night. She'd always liked dancing but couldn't remember the last time she'd done so. Dionne had never taken her out dancing. His idea of a good date was her preparing him dinner at her place. Since their breakup she had analyzed their relationship and knew exactly where they had gone wrong. In Dionne's mind he had been the king and she had been his queen who was supposed to cater to his every whim.

"Renee?"

Tag's voice pulled her thoughts from the past. She smiled. "Yes, Tag, I'll dance with you."

Moments later Tag led her out on the dance floor among all the other couples. She could feel a lot of eyes on them but at the moment she didn't care. All she wanted to think about was Tag, and being surrounded by his kindness, his strength and his warmth. And when he gathered her in his arms, every reason she thought they couldn't be together like this floated from her mind. When he pulled her even closer she seemed to melt against him and an involuntary shudder passed through her body.

"You're cold?" he asked, leaning down and whispering the question in her ear.

She shook her head. "No, I'm not cold." There was no way she could tell him that she was just the opposite. Her insides were burning up with a heat that she'd recently discovered only he could generate.

Renee shifted her attention away from Tag to the dining area filled with smartly dressed couples enjoying their meals. Her gaze lit on one couple in particular when the woman leaned over and whispered something in her husband's ear before turning back and staring at Renee and Tag, frowning deeply. She could only imagine what the woman said since her husband was now staring at them with an equally fierce and disapproving look. Evidently they didn't approve of interracial dating.

Not wanting to see their scornful glares anymore, Renee turned and buried her face in Tag's chest and he pulled her tighter to him as the music swirled around them. She refused to let anyone put a damper on things. Tonight was her and Tag's night and she intended to enjoy it.

She sighed contentedly when she felt his warm and tender hands move from around her waist to the center of her back. He leaned down and began humming the tune that the band was playing. She thought he had one hell of a sexy voice.

The ship made its way to shore and after a couple more dances he took her hand in his. He brought it to his lips. "I hope you enjoyed your evening, Renee."

A quiver passed through her. "I did. Everything was perfect."

He smiled. His gaze was intent when he said, "You

were the most perfect thing here tonight and I'm proud that you were with me and no one else."

Renee couldn't help but smile. If he was using all his skill at that moment to set her up for seduction later, he was doing a good job of it. "And I'm glad I'm here tonight with you, as well."

His gaze held hers for a long moment before he took her hand and led her through the crowd. "I want us to be the first ones off this ship," he said, leading her back to the table. "Our night is far from over yet and with tomorrow being Saturday, just imagine all the possibilities."

She did imagine them and doing so only made her fall in love with him that much more.

Eight

Renee sank into the soft leather cushions of Tag's sofa and focused her gaze on him. He was standing across the room in front of a wall-to-wall entertainment system, and the moment he'd pressed a button, soft jazz music filled the air surrounding them.

She glanced around and saw a number of Alton Malone paintings on his wall as well as paintings from other artists. All beautiful. All expensive. But then his condo, being in Tribeca, had to be up there in the high price range. The wine oak furniture was tasteful and blended well with the modern contemporary decor.

Besides the framed Malone paintings, the living room was decorated with several Asian figurines. Tag had indicated they had been gifts from the Watari Museum in Tokyo after he had done an article about it in *Pulse* a few years ago.

Tag had given her a brief tour of the downstairs but hadn't bothered showing her where his bedroom was. She was rather anxious to see it but when the time was right tonight, there was no doubt in her mind that she would.

Given the heat that had generated off them, between them and with them all evening, a visit to his bedroom was inevitable. After what they had shared last night, she was looking forward to it.

When he had whisked her away from the docks and into his car he had asked if she would like to spend a little time over at his place. She had come close to refusing, remembering the cold, disapproving look the couple had given them on board the ship, but then had decided that tonight she wanted to spend as much time with Tag as possible, and when he took her home later she would explain to him why they couldn't see each other again.

"Would you like something to drink?"

He reclaimed her attention and she met his gaze. Her breath caught. The lamp's light seemed to enhance the vividness of his eyes and the blue was so deep that for a moment it seemed like she was drowning in the ocean. "No, I don't want anything to drink."

"And what do you want?"

Renee was silent. There wasn't an answer she felt comfortable in saying out loud. The silence that drifted between them was tangible, as potent and hot as the very air they were breathing. It didn't take much to recall last night and the way his body had taken hers, had gone deep inside of her, thrusting in and out. Then there was his mouth that had acquainted her with a warm, succulent sweetness that would have her licking her lips for days, nights. And last but not least was the memory of his hands and the way they had glided over her skin, touching places that made ripples of sensation start deep in her abdomen and spread to other parts of her body.

"Renee?"

She continued to hold his gaze, hearing the sound of his voice, strained, husky and filled with something else. Urgency. Need. "Why don't you find out what I want," she said softly, invitingly. She then deliberately took the tip of her tongue and traced her lips, knowing what watching her was doing to him.

She licked steadily as she stared into his tense face. Blatant need shone in the depths of his eyes. Her gaze moved lower, past his tightly muscled stomach to the crotch of his pants, and she saw the erection that strained against the zipper. She suddenly felt hot, and the ventilation from the air conditioning was doing nothing to cool off her heated flesh.

"I think I will."

She shifted her gaze back up to his face as he slowly moved toward her with a smile that sent her pulse racing. "You will what? Find out what I want?"

"No, seduce you into telling me."

Instead of joining her on the sofa he pulled her up and settled her body against his, to feel his hardness. Eyes locked to hers, he whispered huskily, "I want you, Renee."

"And I want you, too, Tag."

As if her words were the go-ahead he had been waiting for, he leaned down and his mouth covered hers in a hungry, desperate, ravenous kiss that had Renee moaning in need when he abruptly ended it.

Questioning eyes met his and he smiled and reached out and tenderly caressed her cheek. "I want you to tell me what you want, sweetheart. Your wish will be my command."

Renee drew in a ragged breath, not being able to imagine such a thing. She'd never had anyone cater exclusively to her needs while they made love. She'd never met anyone like Tag before. Telling him what she wanted and him actually carrying out each and every fantasy she had was an incredibly erotic thought.

"Tell me," he repeated.

She met his gaze and said, "For starters, take me to your bedroom and undress me."

Renee saw his blue eyes go hot just seconds before he bent and gathered her into his arms to carry her up the stairs. Her stomach quivered with the excitement of what would happen when they got to his bedroom. Even now, while they were in motion, she caught his scent. Masculine. Robust. Sexy.

When they entered his bedroom she glanced around. His bed, king-sized with a black platinum steel frame, sat in the center of the room with matching nightstands on each side. A dresser and chest were on the other side of the room. The bedroom reminded her of Tag. Neat, manly and with everything in order.

"Now to remove this dress."

He lowered her down his body and immediately went to work at removing her dress, easing down the zipper as his fingers grazed the warm flesh of her bare back. She wasn't wearing a bra. He moved the soft fabric down her shoulders to drop in a heap at her feet, his gaze locked on the breasts he had grown quite fond of the night before.

"Taste them again, Tag."

She didn't have to ask twice. His tongue flicked out and captured a budding nipple into his mouth. When he heard her moan and felt her knees weaken, he reached out and caught her by the waist. He remembered the orgasm she had the last time he had made love to her breasts, but this time he wanted to prolong her enjoyment, make her want him as much as he wanted her.

He gathered her into his arms and carried her over to the bed and placed her on her back, then lifted her hips to slide the panty hose and thong off of her. Driven by a desire whose depth he couldn't understand, he felt compelled to touch her and instinctively his fingers went to the damp curls between her legs.

She closed her eyes as he focused his concentration on pleasuring her with fingers that stroked her mercilessly. He watched as her lips parted slightly and she moaned out her gratification, while her heavy breathing pleaded with him to quench her desire.

"Too soon, sweetheart," he said, pulling back to remove his own clothes.

When she opened her eyes to watch him they were hot, dark and dilated. He didn't waste time as he tore off his shirt and eased his pants down his legs. With his gaze still locked with hers, he began removing his briefs and once he stood naked in front of the bed, her concentration shifted from his face down to his erection.

"Tell me what you want now," he said, his control almost shot to hell. Anticipation was killing him but he was determined to give her everything she wanted.

"I want you inside of me," she whispered before lying back on his thick bedspread.

The darkness of her skin was a stark contrast to the beige coverlet and he thought it was a breathtaking sight. Not wanting to waste any more time, he quickly pulled a condom out of his nightstand drawer. He kept them there although he'd never used them since Renee was the first woman he'd ever brought home with him. Before, it had been his companion's place or no place. He always considered his condo private and never wanted the memory of a woman's presence there. But with Renee he felt differently. He wanted her memory. He wanted her presence. Point-blank, he wanted her.

He knelt beside her on the bed, eager to join their bodies. He took her mouth again in a deep, hungry kiss, the only kind he shared with her. He knew he had to make love to her right then and pulled back to position his body over hers, and just like the contrast of her skin with his bedspread, he noted the same distinction with his skin. The only word he could think to describe the difference in their coloring was *beautiful.*

He broke off the kiss and looked down into her dark brown eyes. "Ready, sweetheart?"

She smiled up at him. "Only for you."

Her words, whispered seductively, released a surge of heat within him, and clenching his teeth he entered her in one smooth thrust. He breathed in deeply, inhaling her body's sensuous scent, and she arched her back, taking him deeper still, clutching him tightly with her womanly muscles, just as she'd done the last time. And just as before, he could only take so much of her agonizing torture.

Tag felt himself on the brink of tumbling over the edge and knew he had to move. He began setting a rhythm, first by starting a slow rocking motion and then thrusting in and out of her, glorying in the perfect fit they made. With each surge into her body he stoked the fires blazing between them and with each retreat he rekindled them all over again. All he could concentrate on was the woman beneath him, how they seemed made for each other. He called out her name each and every time her muscles clenched pleasure out of him, demanding he give more.

And he did.

An orgasm so intense that it shook his entire body tore through him the exact moment she screamed his name and her body bucked beneath him. He suddenly lost awareness of everything except Renee.

With one last hard thrust, he groaned as he felt her shudder beneath him.

As ecstasy slowly gave way to sweet contentment, he shifted his body, but remained buried deep inside of her, not ready to sever their intimate connection. They faced each other, gazed into each other's eyes as each of their limbs slowly became warm, heavy, pleasured.

Tag looked at her in amazement, thinking that Renee Williams was definitely what dreams were made of. He leaned closer and gently kissed her, needing to taste her, to absorb her, to appreciate her. And to thank the powers that had brought this beautiful woman into his life.

After Tag finished getting dressed he turned to watch Renee slip back into her dress. He stared at her for a long, thoughtful moment and a feeling he had never experienced before tugged at his heart, kicking his pulse into high gear.

The passion between them was fiery, breathtaking, but he didn't just want her sexually. He also enjoyed doing things with her, spending time with her, taking her places and sharing his thoughts with her. Tonight over dinner he had told her about his work and the challenges he, his father and brother at *Pulse* were facing trying to compete against the other three magazines. She had listened, hung on to his every word and then she had made several comments that had made him think.

Renee had pointed out that if his grandfather's challenge was making them tense, then imagine what it was doing to the people who worked for them. Were they worried about what would happen to their jobs if the magazine they worked for didn't make a good enough profit? And what changes in the corporate structure would the new CEO make? Changes in corporate dynamics could send workers into a panic and could result in a serious employer-employee relationship problem.

He knew her comments had only been the result of her innate concern for people. She was a person who cared about how people were treated, how a person felt and what a person thought. The latter, he sighed deeply, was the root of their problem, and the very reason she continued to put a roadblock in the way of a developing relationship between them. Tension rippled off him in acknowledging how far apart they still were on the issue of them getting together. They needed to talk.

He leaned against his dresser and watched as she struggled with the zipper on her dress. He liked her outfit. The sexy black dress fit her as if it had been made for her body alone, and the ruffles at the hem showed off a pair of truly gorgeous legs. He felt as though he could stand there and stare at her forever. "Need help?" he finally asked when her attempts at the zipper proved futile.

She shot him a look over her shoulder and smiled. "Only if you'll help me get it up."

He chuckled as he crossed the room to her. "Oh, I think that can be arranged." He easily slid up her zipper then reached around and wrapped his arms around her waist, pulling her back to him, liking the feel of her butt resting against his groin.

"Are you sure I can't convince you to spend the night?" he leaned down and prodded softly in her ear. "I promise to make it worth your while."

Renee sighed deeply and leaned back farther against Tag, luxuriating in the feel of his arms around her. More than anything she wanted to spend the night, to wake up beside him in the morning, like they had the previous night. But she knew that doing so would only make it that much harder to walk away and not look back.

"No, Tag, I don't think my spending the night here will be wise," she said with a shake of her head.

"Why?" he asked, turning her around to face him, although he already knew her argument. But tonight he was ready for it. His gaze locked with hers. "Explain to me why you won't spend the night."

She raised her eyes to the ceiling. "What will your neighbors think when they see me?"

"That I'm one hell of a lucky man."

Renee sighed. Everything about tonight had been beautiful and she didn't want to shatter the enchanted moments, but she had to make him understand. "Not everyone will think that, Tag. There will be some who will not like the fact we're dating."

He frowned and crossed his arms over his chest. "Then I'd say it's their problem and not ours."

Renee shook her head. "What about your family?"

He remembered she had brought up his family before. "I thought I had made things perfectly clear about my family. They don't and won't dictate who I see."

Renee crossed her arms over her own chest and lifted her chin. "No, but they would be concerned. I can't see the public-conscious Elliotts welcoming an African-American into their fold. You even said tonight how your grandfather has always drilled into all of your heads never to do anything unsavory regarding your family name."

Tag's frown deepened. "And you see our dating as unsavory?"

"I don't but there are others who would." She could clearly remember what had happened the last time her name was linked to gossip. It hadn't been a good feeling knowing she was the hot topic of everyone's conversations.

Frustrated, Tag rubbed his hand against the back of his neck. "Don't you think you're blowing this out of proportion, Renee? Almost everywhere you go these days you encounter mixed-race couples. This is New York, for heaven's sake. How about stepping back into the real world and looking around you? Notice the social trend that's evolving. The mainstream of American society isn't concerned about mixed couples anymore. They have a lot more to worry about, like the economy, making sure our country is kept safe, healthy and free. That's what's on their minds, Renee, and not who's crossing racial lines."

"For your information, Teagan Elliott, there are many people in the real world who do care about who's crossing racial lines."

"And you want to give in to them?"

Renee drew her head back and glared up at Tag. "It's not giving in to them."

"Then what do you call it? I like you. You like me. Yet you don't want to date me because of what people might think or say? I call that giving in to a segment of society who can't move on and accept people as people and not attach a color to them."

"Maybe one day things will be different but—"

"I don't want to wait for one day, Renee. The only thing I want is today, this moment. I don't give a damn that your skin is darker than mine. What's important is that I care for you. I want to be with you, get to know you better, spend time with you. And I want you to get to know me. And the more you get to know me the more you'll see that I am my own man. I make my own decisions. I choose my own woman."

He reached out his hand to her. "Will you give me a chance? Will you give *us* a chance?" A smile touched the corners of his lips. "You're a very beautiful woman and personally, I don't think I'm such a bad catch. What do you think?"

At that moment Renee thought her heart would swell over with the love she felt for this man standing before her. She stared into his blue eyes and saw the sincerity shining in their depths. "I think," she said in a somewhat shaky voice as she took the hand he offered, "that you've presented a very good argument."

"And?" he asked, drawing her closer to him. She came to him willingly, which to Tag was a good sign. She smiled while placing her palms against his chest, which, in his book, was another good sign. His heart rate increased and he felt his blood thicken in his veins.

"And," she said, taking another step closer to him, molding her body against his and igniting an inferno within him, "I think that we'll try things your way and see what happens."

"I can tell you what's going to happen," he said in a quiet voice, lowering his head toward hers.

"And just what do you predict?" she asked, rising on tiptoes to meet him.

"I predict that one day we're going to wonder why we even had this argument."

Renee opened her mouth to disagree, but his mouth

came down on hers, effectively kissing away any words she was about to say. Sensation ripped through her when he parted her lips with his tongue and claimed the depths of what awaited him inside.

Moments later he tore his mouth free of hers just long enough to whisper, "Will you stay the night with me?"

"Yes," she murmured through kiss-swollen lips. "I'll stay."

He smiled and kissed her again as his hands eased around to her back and slowly began unzipping the dress that he had zipped up earlier.

Nine

Gannon snapped his fingers in front of Tag's face. "Hey, Tag, are you with us?"

Tag snapped out of his reverie and blinked. He looked first at Gannon and then at Erika, Liam and Bridget. All four had silly grins on their faces at having caught the ever-alert Teagan Elliott daydreaming.

They were sitting in the living room in The Tides, his grandparents' primary place of residence, and where his mother was currently convalescing. As a child he'd loved visiting his grandparents here. Situated on five acres on a bluff above the Atlantic Ocean, the Elliotts' compound had its own private, guarded road. On the estate was the house, a large pool, the pool house, a beautiful English rose garden and a helicopter landing pad. The feature he loved the most was the hand-carved stone staircase that led down the bluff to a private beach with a boat dock. It was from that dock that his father and grandfather had taught him how to sail.

"Tag?"

Hearing his brother speak to him a second time, Tag thought he'd better respond. "Yes, I'm with you guys, although I'm getting bored to tears," he said, smiling. "Talk about something that won't put me to sleep, will you?"

Bridget made a face. "Um, how about if we discuss the fact that you were seen at a Broadway play on Saturday night," she said, tipping a glass of wine to her lips.

Tag rolled his eyes, knowing his sister had gotten her information from Caroline Dutton, a high school friend of hers who was known for her loose lips. Everyone knew Caroline was a chip off the old block since her mother, Lila Dutton, was one of the worst gossips anyone could have the misfortune of knowing. He had run into Caroline at the play on Saturday, and if Bridget knew he had gone to the play then she also knew the person he had taken with him.

"Don't hold your breath for that one." Tag leaned back in his chair and smiled. Waking up beside Renee had been a wonderful experience on Saturday morning. After making love again, they had showered together and then he had taken her home to change clothes.

He had talked her into going to see the *Lion King* and they both enjoyed it immensely. Afterwards, he had taken her back to her place and he had spent the night.

"Your smile is downright sickening, Tag."

His smile widened as he glanced over at Liam. "Is it? Sorry." He knew everyone was curious but he had no intention of sharing the reason for his blissful contentment with anyone.

"Dinner is ready to be served."

Tag stood, grateful for Olive's timely announcement. Olive and her husband, Benjamin, had worked for his grandparents for years as The Tides' main caretakers. Olive, at fifty-five, was the housekeeper and Ben, at fifty-seven, was the groundskeeper. Both ran their own staffs and kept things orderly.

"When will Mother be coming down?" he hung back and asked when the others had left the room.

"She's on her way now," Olive said, smiling brightly. "Whoever's idea it was for her to help with Gannon and Erika's wedding definitely had the right idea. Her mood has improved dramatically."

Tag was glad to hear that. He had been worried that at some point she might start withdrawing again. "I'm anxious to see her." He hadn't seen her since before she'd been released from the hospital.

"And I know she's anxious to see all of you as well. The last few weeks have been difficult for her."

Tag shook his head. "When do you expect my grandparents to return?" He knew they had taken a pleasure trip to Florida to meet with other couples that belonged to the Irish American Historical Society.

"By the end of next week, in time for Gannon's wedding and to get things ready for their anniversary dinner. They call every day to check how your mom is doing and be sure she gets all the rest she needs before she begins her chemotherapy treatments."

Tag sighed and traced his hand down his face. He

tried not to think about that additional phase in his mother's recovery. When he heard voices he walked out into the foyer and glanced in the direction of the staircase. His parents were standing together on the top stair and whatever his father had told his mother had made her smile.

Although she looked somewhat pale and exhausted, there was a part of her fighting for the sparkle and glow to come through. He'd noticed more than once that his father had the ability to bring out that sparkle by coaxing her into a smile with whatever private words he would tell her.

A part of Tag admired what his parents had shared for over thirty years and for the first time in his life he knew that one day he wanted that same thing for himself. The chance to share his life with someone who would not only be his spouse, but his lover and best friend, as well.

"Come on to the kitchen and leave them alone for a little while longer," Olive whispered in his ear.

Tag nodded and followed Olive into the kitchen.

Tag could only be grateful that his mother was doing as well as she was. In a way, dinner was just like old times when they would all share a meal together. But the one thing that was different was that his father hadn't rushed out in the middle of it, thinking there was something at the office he just had to do. Another thing was that after dinner everyone lingered, not in a hurry to leave, and most importantly, his mother was the center of all their attention and concern.

"So how are things going with you, Tag?" his mother asked, sending him a fond smile as they walked together outside on the grounds, her hand firmly anchored to his sleeve, her steps slower than usual.

He looked down at her and smiled. "I'm doing better now that I see that you're doing well." His siblings had left moments earlier and he had remained, needing this time alone with his mother. The two of them had always had a rather close relationship. As a child he'd thought she was beautiful. He still did. And he'd also been convinced that she was the smartest person in the world since any advice she'd always given him had been timely and needed—whether he'd wanted to receive it or not.

"How are things at the office?" she inquired, evidently feeling the need to break her question down further.

Tag let his lips curve, recognizing her strategy. "Work is kind of crazy right now and a part of me is angry at Granddad because of the way things are. Over the years I've felt more than once that some of the decisions he has made were based more on keeping up appearances than putting his family first, but I think this recent antic of his is a real doozy. I can't imagine what he was thinking. Dad is the eldest, so when Granddad retires, he should rightfully become CEO. Everyone expected it, so I just don't get it."

Karen nodded in understanding. "At the moment none of us do, Tag. I think Patrick's decision hurt Michael somewhat, but you know your father. He will abide by your grandfather's wishes."

Karen stopped walking for a moment and looked up

at Tag, fixing her dark eyes on his. "So now, tell me, how are things going in your personal life?"

Tag was acutely aware that his mother, in her own way, was probing. And although she'd always been curious about his personal life, she'd kept the pointed questions to a minimum. For some reason he felt she was asking out of more than polite curiosity and quickly wondered if someone had mentioned something to her. One of his siblings? His father?

He couldn't help but recall that day in the hospital waiting room when he had referred to Renee by her first name and his father had given him that surprised look. One thing Tag had discovered while growing up was that Michael Elliott was not slow. He caught on quickly. Dismissing the thought that the informant was one of his siblings, Tag concluded his father had said something.

He met his mother's gaze and smiled, deciding to be completely honest, the only way he could be with her. "My personal life is going great, although I was having problems with this certain young lady not taking me seriously, but I've finally convinced her otherwise."

"Is it Renee?"

Tag lifted a brow, knowing it was as he'd suspected. His father *had* told her. His smile widened as he answered, deciding not to question how she knew. It was enough that she did. "Yes, it's Renee. We're seeing each other."

Karen smiled. "She's a beautiful girl and I know firsthand how genuinely caring she is. She helped me through a difficult time and for that I'm most grateful.

There's something so uniquely elegant about her and I can't help but notice how she goes out of her way to help someone. I think she's good for you and that the two of you would make a beautiful couple."

After a brief moment of silence, she said, "Earlier, you mentioned something about Renee not taking you seriously. Does that mean she's not fully accepting of sharing a relationship with you?"

Tag chuckled, thinking that was one way to put it. "She was pretty reluctant at first but she's slowly beginning to thaw. I've gotten her to at least agree to give us a chance to see where things will go. Because we're an interracial couple she's concerned about what people will say."

"The family?"

"Yes, among others. We've garnered our share of frowns and stares whenever we're seen together. I can ignore them a lot better than she can."

Karen nodded. "As far as the family's acceptance, I don't think you'll have any problems, however, you know your grandfather. He can take protecting the family's name to uncompromising heights."

Tag frowned, controlling the quick surge of anger that consumed him at the mere thought. "Yes, and when the time comes I will deal with him about this if I have to. Under no circumstances will I let him, or anyone, dictate how I spend my life and with whom."

Karen looked at her son, feeling his resentment. "I'd like to offer some words of advice, if I may."

"Certainly." Although she had asked, Tag knew she would give her advice anyway.

"Since finding out about my cancer I've discovered just how little time we have on this earth to do the things we want to do, to be with the person or people we want to be with. It's made me realize one very important thing and that is nothing, and I mean nothing—not prestige, power or pride—is worth sacrificing the things that you truly want, the things that you truly love.

"Don't be afraid to take time and smell the roses. Don't hesitate in seeking out those things you hold dear. Seeking them out and holding on to them. And don't ever cease standing up for what you believe in, and fighting for those things that you want. Life is too short. Do what makes you happy, regardless of how others might feel. Do what makes Tag happy."

Tag sighed deeply. He smiled, thinking his mother was still the smart woman he'd always thought her to be. He lifted her hand to his lips. "Thanks for the advice. I intend to take it."

"So, how was your mom?" Renee asked as she sank onto the edge of her sofa. As soon as the phone rang she had gotten this excited feeling in the pit of her stomach. For some reason she had known it would be Tag.

"Considering all she's been through I think her spirits are rather high. Her health seems to be improving each day and she's getting around a lot better."

"That's good."

"And she's excited about the plans for Gannon and Erika's wedding, although she understands they want it to be a small affair with just family. Dad says Mom has been busy on the phone with caterers and florists, and

I can tell just from talking to her that she's really enjoying it."

There was a pause, and then he said, "Mom and I got a chance to spend some time alone and I told her that you and I were seeing each other."

An uneasy shiver crept up Renee's spine. "You did?"

"Yes."

"And what did she say?" she asked, trying to keep her voice even.

"She smiled and said she thought we made a nice couple."

Renee arched her brow. "Was that the only thing she said?"

"No. She also told me how much she liked you and how much you had helped her through a difficult time. She actually thinks you're good for me."

A jitter of happiness shot through Renee. She couldn't help but smile. "Did she really say that?"

"Yes, and those were her exact words."

Renee sighed. "Thanks for sharing that with me."

"I'd like to share a whole lot more."

She shook her head, grinning as she thought of all they'd shared that weekend, especially the intensity with which he had made love to her. "Haven't you shared enough?"

"You haven't seen anything yet. I'd like to make plans for us for this Tuesday night. Would you go out with me?"

"Tuesday?"

"Yes, it's Valentine's Day."

"Oh." She hadn't had a reason to celebrate Valentine's Day in so long that she'd forgotten. "And you want to take me out?"

"Of course. I want to plan a special evening just for you."

Renee shifted her body on the cushions of her sofa. "Are you sure?"

Tag laughed. "Of course I'm sure. There's no one else I'd rather spend such a special day with. Will it be okay to pick you up around seven?"

She sighed deeply, remembering the decision they had made. "Yes, seven will be fine. Any particular way I should dress?"

"It's a semiformal affair. One of my mother's favorite charities, the Heart Association, is holding its annual Heart to Heart Ball."

Renee swallowed. That meant a lot of people would be attending. She was just coming to terms with her decision that she and Tag give things a try. She wasn't sure if she was ready to handle something of this magnitude. Panic rose within her. The last thing she wanted to do was to give people something to talk about. "Tag?"

"Yes, sweetheart?"

His endearment caused a sudden calming effect to settle over her. She would do as she promised and give them a chance. "Nothing. I'll see you on Tuesday."

"I can't wait."

She smiled. "Neither can I. Good-night."

As soon as she ended their call she placed her arms across her stomach when it began to feel tense. No, she wouldn't give in to any panic attacks. For now she would follow her heart and see where it led.

* * *

"So what do you think, Erika?" Tag asked.

Erika pursed her lips and sighed. She glanced across the *Pulse* conference room at Gannon, Tag and Marlene Kingston, then leaned back in her chair and smiled. "I think an excellent job was done with this article and that we should definitely make it our cover story."

Gannon lifted a brow. "In next month's issue?"

Erika shook her head. "No. I suggest we go to a special edition. If we sit on this story we run the risk of *Time* doing it first. You can't convince me that sooner or later someone won't get suspicious about Senator Denton's resignation like we did and start digging."

Tag nodded. "Okay then, we're in agreement," he said excitedly. He turned to Marlene. "And I'll add my kudos to Erika's for a well-written story."

"Thanks," Marlene said beaming. "I appreciate you giving me the opportunity to do it."

After Marlene left, Erika lifted an eyebrow and asked, "Where's Peter?"

Gannon sighed. "I don't know. This is another important meeting that he's missed." No one said anything, but Tag knew his brother was being forced to deal with an issue that he'd been avoiding. Peter Weston was simply not pulling his weight.

Tag stood. "All right then, it's all settled," he said excitedly. "Let the presses roll and let's watch the sales flow in."

Later that evening Tag joined Liam, Bridget and his cousin Scarlet at Une Nuit. Despite everyone's smiles he could feel tension at the table the moment he sat down. "What's going on?"

Releasing an affronted sigh his sister said, "Nothing, other than that earlier today I saw Cullen at the office and asked him how things were going at *Snap* and he almost bit my head off. You would have thought I was asking him for some deep, dark secret."

"Personally, I think Grandfather's challenge has got all of you on guard," Bryan said, in defense of his younger brother as he pulled up a chair and joined them. "That's why I'm glad I got out of the family business and started this place. Even then there was too much pressure at EPH. I don't want to think how crazy things are now."

Tag nodded. "Bryan is right. Granddad's challenge has all of us tense. We've always worked together for the good of the company as a whole and have never been pitted against each other like this before. But we can't lose sight that no matter what, we're family."

Liam took a sip of his drink. "I agree with Tag."

Scarlet rolled her eyes, grinning. "You would, since your job as financial operating officer doesn't align you with any particular magazine."

Liam frowned. "Yes, but it doesn't make my job easier when I have to do damage control with all four. Try doing my job."

"No, brother dear, you can keep your job," Bridget said. "I don't know of anyone who could do it better. It's just that things are getting crazy already, just like Bryan said, and it's only the second month. I don't want to think what the summer will bring when things really begin to heat up."

Bridget then glanced over at Scarlet. "And speaking of Summer…where is she?" she asked Scarlet regarding the whereabouts of her identical twin.

Scarlet took a sip of her drink before saying, "Summer's excited about John returning to town in time for the ball tomorrow night and decided to go shopping for something to wear."

Bridget smiled. "I'm glad that I'm not the only one who's looking forward to the ball tomorrow night."

Tag leaned back in his chair and thought of the evening he had planned with Renee and said, "I'm looking forward to the ball tomorrow night, as well."

Renee looked in the full-length mirror that was on the back of her bathroom door, not believing the transformation a visit to the hair salon and an exclusive dress boutique could make. But she wanted to look as special as Tag had promised the night would be.

The day had started off promisingly when a prettily wrapped cookie bouquet was delivered to her at work. She had gotten a curious stare from Vicki, but as usual, her secretary had respected her privacy by not asking any questions. Tag's card had simply said, *Be My Valentine.*

Then when she'd gotten home there had been the delivery of the Malone painting she had fallen in love with that Saturday she and Tag had spent together in Greenwich Village. She didn't want to think how much Tag had paid for the painting and her first reaction was that there was no way she could accept it. But when she'd finally reached him on his cell he'd told her there was no way she could return the painting; it was hers to keep. He then bid her goodbye, promising to see her at seven.

She chuckled as she tossed her hair from her face. Instead of the straight strands she usually wore, her hair was a silken mass of curls that framed her face and tumbled around her shoulders.

She stepped back to study the effect of the semi-formal dress she had purchased to wear. Made of red velvet, it looked sophisticated, chic, tailored to fit. Matte sequins dotted the v-neck that emphasized her high, full breasts, accentuated even more by delicate spaghetti straps. The soft fluttery hemline stopped just above her knees.

The way the dress flowed over her body elegantly displayed every feminine curve she possessed, and the glamorous matching red velvet cape, lined with white satin, was a plus to keep the tonight's chill at bay. She wished that her friend Debbie were here to give her a thumbs-up, but Debbie wouldn't be back in New York until Saturday.

When the doorbell sounded, Renee's pulse jumped before she took a quick glance at her watch. It was precisely seven o'clock.

The lady in red…

Tag's gaze moved with deep male appreciation over Renee's stunning features. In the gorgeous gown she was wearing, she was definitely making a statement tonight, and he was glad he was the man whose arm she would be on.

"You are beautiful," he said, stepping inside her apartment and handing her a single red rose.

"Thank you." Renee brought the rose to her nose and inhaled softly. She then took in the man standing in front of her. There was just something about a good-looking man in formal attire. Tag was elegantly dressed in a black tux that fit his tall, muscular frame as if it had been specifically tailored just for him. She smiled thinking that it probably had been. The white shirt and formal black bow tie added the finishing touches. "I think you are beautiful, too," she said, meaning every word of it.

A slow smile spread across his features. "I don't think I've ever been told that I'm beautiful."

"Well, I'm telling you," she said, bringing the rose to her nose once again. The blue eyes holding hers were igniting a slow burn inside of her. She had a feeling if they didn't leave now they would arrive at the ball inappropriately late.

"Ready to leave?" she decided to ask.

A grin touched the corners of his mouth and she had a feeling he had read her every thought. "Yes, I think we'd better."

The first thing Renee noted when they arrived at the Rockefeller Center was that the main entrance was surrounded by the media. Television cameras, newspaper reporters and photographers were positioned close to the main entrance, which was lined with red carpet.

"Because of the importance of this event, a number

of celebrities will be in attendance," Tag whispered in her ear just moments before she saw John Travolta and his wife entering the establishment as flashbulbs exploded everywhere.

Renee nodded, already feeling nervous. She had never been to a ball before, nor could she recall ever having been in a limo. Tag had surprised her when he'd shown up at her apartment in a limousine, giving her neighbors a reason to raise their blinds in the evening.

When the limo came to a stop in front of Rockefeller Center, a uniformed doorman stepped forward and opened the door for them. The moment they exited the vehicle, flashbulbs went off. Evidently, someone had assumed they were celebrities. Renee felt good knowing that once it was discovered they weren't anyone famous, the photos would be disposed of. She smiled up at Tag when he took her arm, and together they walked into the building.

The first people she recognized upon entering the ballroom were Gannon and Erika. For some reason, the couple didn't appear surprised that she was Tag's date tonight.

"Doesn't this place look fabulous?" Erika said. "Whoever was responsible for the decorating did a wonderful job."

Renee nodded. She had to agree. With Valentine colors of red and white, everything was reminiscent of love and romance. It was there in the red and white carnations that seemed to be practically everywhere and in the red heart-shaped ceramic centerpieces that adorned the tables that were draped in red and white linen tablecloths. Then there were the bright chandeliers overhead as well as the love song being played by the live orchestra. There was no doubt in her mind there would be dancing later, and a part of her was looking forward to dancing with Tag.

For the next hour or so Renee and Tag walked around, socializing. He kept a hand on her arm, keeping her close by his side as they moved around the room, while introducing her to people he knew. And it seemed that just about everyone knew him as an Elliott and immediately inquired about his mother's health and his grandparents' whereabouts. He answered by saying his mother was recuperating nicely and his grandparents hadn't returned yet from their trip to South Florida.

Dinner was extravagant as well as delicious and Renee was extremely grateful they had been seated at the table with Gannon and Erika as well as with Tag's cousin Cullen and his date. When they had spent the weekend together, Tag had told her a little bit about each of his siblings and cousins and she distinctively remembered him saying that Cullen, at twenty-seven, was the playboy in the family. With his dark, good looks she could tell why. But then, she thought, glancing over at her date, no one was more handsome than Tag.

"Dance with me," Tag whispered in her ear once the dance floor opened. She nodded, and without any hesitation she let him lead her to the dance floor.

He slid his arms around her waist, bringing her closer to the fit of him, and she went willingly, deciding that so far tonight everything had been perfect. There were even enough celebrities in attendance to take everyone's attention off her and Tag.

"Thanks for coming with me tonight," he said softly, leaning down as his warm lips gently touched her ear.

His amorous caress sent chills of desire escalating through her body. "Thank you for inviting me."

He chuckled quietly. "There we go again, thanking each other like broken records. If we were alone I would take the time to thank you properly."

She glanced up at him and gave him a jaunty grin. "And which way is that?"

He leaned closer and whispered, telling her of his fondest desire for later. Renee chuckled softly and said, "It's a good thing I don't embarrass easily."

"Yes, it is a good thing."

After the dance was over he was leading her back to their table when someone called out his name.

They turned just in time for a woman to fling herself into Tag's arms and kiss him on the mouth with a familiarity that made Renee blink. "Where on earth have you been keeping yourself, Tag? I haven't seen you for months."

"Hello, Pamela," he said with a dry smile. Reaching out, he pulled Renee closer to his side. "Renee, I'd like you to meet Pamela Hoover, an old friend," Tag said as a way of introduction.

"Hello," the woman said coldly, then turned her full attention back to Tag. Dismissing Renee completely, she said, "What are you doing Friday night? I have tickets to—"

Tag interrupted her. "Sorry, but Renee and I have plans for Friday night."

Although Renee knew that she and Tag really didn't have a date Friday night, she decided not to mention that fact.

"Oh." The woman then gave Renee an unfriendly glance before turning back to Tag. "Then perhaps we can get together another day, for old times' sake. You know my number." She then walked off.

Evidently, Tag felt the need to explain. "Pamela and I dated over a year ago. When she didn't like competing against my work, we decided things weren't working out and went our separate ways."

"Oh, I see." Renee decided not to tell him that what she saw was someone very much interested in rekindling what they once had.

"There're a few people I know over there. Let's go over and say hello," Tag said, leading her across the room.

Moments later Renee found herself surrounded by a number of famous people, most of whose movies she enjoyed watching on the big screen. And Tag was on a first-name basis with each and every one of them. She ignored the feeling of being way out of her league since everyone appeared to be genuinely friendly.

"I figured I would see you here tonight," said a man who walked up behind Tag.

Tag turned at the sound of the voice and smiled. "And I was hoping I'd see you." He pulled Renee closer to his side to make introductions. "Renee, this is a good friend of mine, Alton Malone."

Renee smiled as she presented the man her hand.

"Mr. Malone, Tag never mentioned that you were a good friend of his."

Alton laughed, shaking his head. "Then I will definitely take him to task for that, Renee. I understand you like my work."

"Yes, I do, and I was happy to receive a special painting of yours today as a gift."

"Then I hope you can come to the private art exhibit I have planned this Friday night at a museum in Harlem."

Renee glanced over at Tag, wondering if this was the date he'd earlier insinuated they had. His mischievous smile let her know it was. She nodded her head, grinning. "Thanks, Alton, and I think I will."

A half hour later Renee excused herself from Tag's side to go to the ladies' room. She was about to enter when a very distinct voice from the inside stopped her.

"Can you believe the nerve of Tag coming here with her?" Pamela asked her unseen companion. "What on earth could he be thinking?"

Another woman laughed. "Yes, I saw them the moment they walked in together. I couldn't believe it."

"Me neither," Pamela tacked on. "I looked for Tag's grandfather to see his reaction and someone mentioned that he's out of town. He's going to croak when he finds out that Tag is dating a black woman. Just think of the talk it's going to cause. The one thing Patrick Elliott detests is his family name being connected to any type of scandal."

Renee stiffened and backed slowly away from the door. Deciding she didn't have an urgent need to use the bathroom after all, she returned to the ballroom.

It didn't take long to find Tag. His tall, elegantly attired form was standing across the room talking to his brother and his cousin, Cullen. And then, as if he were in tune with her very presence, he glanced up and met her eyes.

He made the mistake of letting his gaze linger on her too long. The longer he looked at her, the more she could feel the wanting and desire radiating from the very depths of him. Love for him took over her mind, erasing Pamela Hoover's cutting and spiteful words, and filling Renee's mind with one thought: just how much she loved him.

She watched as he excused himself from the group and without looking around and making conversation with anyone, he strolled over to her as if she was the only person who had his complete attention. She wondered if he was aware of how he stood out—tall, dashing, handsome—and she continued to stare at him. Out of breath. Out of her mind.

When he came to a stop in front of her, she wet her lips, knowing the provocative and sensuous gesture would send him a silent message.

It did.

He slid his arms around her waist and leaned closer, and, not caring who was looking, he placed an affectionate kiss on her lips. "Are you ready to leave now?" he whispered.

She liked the feel of being in his arms, being pressed so close to him. She liked having his attention. "Only if you are."

"I am."

And without any more words, he took her hand and led her toward the coat check to get her cape.

Renee remembered very little of the limo ride back to her apartment. Nor could she recall the moments she and Tag shared as they walked hand in hand to her door. But she did remember when that same door closed behind them and he whispered her name just moments before pulling her into his arms.

And she did commit to memory how he had gently carried her to her bedroom, placed her on the bed and tenderly undressed her before turning his attention to himself.

She would never forget how she watched as he shoved his pants to the floor and stepped out of them, confident in his sexuality. And when he got in the bed with her, knelt before her, spread her legs, lowered his head and flicked his tongue across her womanly core, she thought that she had died and gone to heaven.

By the time he had raised his head, she had had not one orgasm but two and he'd given her a look that let her know that before the night was over there would be a third and a fourth.

"Careful," she whispered, after he sheathed a condom in place and moved his body into position over hers. "You're becoming habit-forming."

He smiled down at her. "I'm glad. I want to get into your system, Renee. I want to get into it real bad."

She reached out and caressed the side of his face. "Why?" she asked, desperately needing to know.

"Because," he said, as he slowly entered her, "you're already in mine."

"Maybe. But not enough."

At that moment she didn't know what was driving her but she wanted to be the only woman Tag thought about tonight, tomorrow, possibly for the rest of his life. Maybe it had something to do with the words Pamela Hoover had spoken, suggesting that once Patrick Elliott got wind of her and Tag's relationship it would all be over. Renee wouldn't subject him to any sort of rift with his family and she knew what she had to do if that became a possibility. But tonight, tomorrow, just for a little while longer, she wanted this. She needed him.

She wrapped her legs securely around him and then she began trailing her fingers down his chest, initiating a slow, seductive massage before coming to a stop on one taut nipple.

"What are you doing?" he asked, his voice hitched to a feverous pitch from her touch.

"I'm trying to see just how deep into your system I can get," she said, stroking the nipple slowly, sensuously.

"Take my word," he said through clenched teeth. "You're already in there pretty good."

"But I want to make sure."

"You know what they say about payback," he said, sucking in a deep breath.

"No, I don't know what they say, but tonight I've decided that I'm not going to worry about what anyone says. The only thing I want on my mind is us and what we're doing right now."

Laughing, she shifted her body and after a quick maneuver Tag found himself on his back with her straddling him.

He looked up at her through deeply glazed eyes. "Oh, you're asking for it."

"From the feel of things it seems like you're the one asking for it, Mr. Elliott, and I intend to give you everything you want."

And then she began to move on top of him.

It suddenly happened, as soon as she felt his body explode beneath her. With his last hard thrust she screamed his name and shattered into a thousand pieces before collapsing on him, burying her head in the hollow of his shoulder.

Moments later, he kissed her deeply, thoroughly and completely, and at that moment Renee knew that instead of her getting deeper into his system he had gotten totally entrenched into hers.

Contentment surged through every part of Tag's body as he stood at the foot of the bed and drank in the sight of Renee lying there asleep atop the covers. Even now, aftershocks of pleasure rushed through his veins, keeping him hard. The intimacy they always shared was unlike anything he'd ever known. She brought out the sexual hunger in him, his wanting and desire were driven to extreme points, and unleashed within him was something so elemental and profound that it took his breath away just thinking about it.

He started to get dressed as he continued to look at her. The woman was something else—stubborn, proud, beautiful and sexy all rolled into one. She matched him on every level. Surpassed him on some. And pleased him with a magnitude that could leave him gasping.

He sighed deeply as he buttoned his shirt. More than anything he wanted to get back in bed and be there when Renee woke up in the morning, but he couldn't. *Pulse*'s special edition would hit the stands tomorrow morning and there was a lot to do. For the next forty-eight hours the majority of his time would be spent at the office. Once the magazine hit the street he would then have to be on hand to field inquiries from those questioning the story's legitimacy.

Wanting to clear his mind of work, he looked back at Renee and did something he had never done before. He began imagining. How would it feel to have this every day, the chance to sleep with her, wake up with her, spend all the time that he wanted with her?

An emotion he had never felt before suddenly gripped him and the one thing he could not imagine was a life without her. He sucked in a sharp breath when he was filled with a deep longing, a profound sense of need. He'd known that he cared, but until now he hadn't realized how much.

He was in love with Renee.

The thought, the blatant realization didn't make him feel uncomfortable. It sent a warmth through all parts of his body, swelling his heart with love even more. Now he imagined other things. Sharing his entire life with her. Marrying her and making her his wife. The mother of his children.

He wanted to wake her up and tell her how he felt but knew that he couldn't. There were still issues they were working out and although she had agreed to give them a chance, he could still sense her wariness, her uncertainty. The best thing for him to do would be to continue on their present path. He had to prove to her that things between them could work out and there was nothing that existed in this world that could keep them apart.

After getting completely dressed he returned to her, leaned down and nibbled her neck. He couldn't leave without telling her goodbye. "I'm getting ready to leave, sweetheart."

She slowly opened her eyes and drew a long, heavy breath before saying, "How? The limo is—"

"I called for a car." EPH had its own private transportation. "It'll be here in a few moments." As he continued to look at her, he realized this woman held his heart and she didn't even know it. He leaned down and kissed her, tenderly yet thoroughly.

With his lips still locked to hers he slipped his hand beneath her knees and picked her up. He then sat on the edge of the bed with her in his lap. He needed the connection. He needed this. The exquisite sensations that only she could force through his body, an unrestrained surrender that only she had been able to seize.

He reluctantly lifted his mouth sometime later, only after he was thoroughly satisfied that he had given her something to think about for the next few days when he would be so busy with the magazine.

"That special edition comes out tomorrow," he said hoarsely, placing small kisses around her lips. "I need to be in place."

"I know," she said quietly.

"I'm going to be busy over the next couple of days. I probably won't get a chance to see you until Friday night."

She slid her hand up his shirt, straightened his bow tie and whispered, "I understand."

"I'm going to miss you."

She smiled up at him. "I'm going to miss you, too."

Taking advantage of her parted lips, he slipped his tongue back inside her mouth for one last, sweet, mind-stirring taste. Moments later, with a low groan, he pulled back, stood and placed her back in bed. "If I don't leave now, I won't."

"I know that as well."

He held her gaze for a moment, and then took his cell phone out of the pocket of his pants. Somehow in the midst of his whirling senses he was able to press a few buttons, and when the dispatcher came on the line, he said tensely, "Delay that pickup in Morningside Heights for another couple of hours." He clicked off the phone and placed it aside, then began removing his clothes.

Unrestrained. Uncontrolled. He was a man very much in love and once again he wanted the woman, the object of his desire, the person who held his heart. He wanted to make love to her with the knowledge that love was guiding his thoughts, his actions and his words.

When he was completely naked, he joined Renee in bed, knowing that at that moment, this was where he wanted to be.

Ten

When Renee walked through the doors of Manhattan University Hospital that morning she had the eerie feeling of being watched. It seemed that everyone's eyes were on her, and a number of speculative faces turned to stare at her when she made her usual trek across the lobby before stepping into the elevator.

Hoping that that she was imagining things, she walked out onto her floor moments later only to see Vicki look up from her desk and stare at her as well. "Okay, I give up," Renee said, after hanging up her coat and walking over to Vicki's desk. "What's going on?"

"I take it you haven't seen this morning's paper," her secretary said, easing the tabloid across the desk to her.

Renee lifted a brow before glancing down at the paper. Her heart nearly stopped. There, plastered on the front page, were pictures from the ball, and dead center were two pictures of her and Tag. The first was a photograph of them getting out of the limo together, making all of New York aware of the fact that she had been his date. The other photo was taken when he had leaned down to kiss her—the moment right before they had left the ball. Beneath the pictures the caption asked, Has the Elusive Teagan Elliott Finally Been Caught?

Renee swallowed. She hadn't wanted her relationship with Tag exposed to the world this way, especially while it wasn't yet on solid ground. "With all the other stuff going on in this country, I wouldn't think the ball warranted front page," she said, not knowing at the moment what else to say.

Vicki shrugged. "Yes, you would think not." She then added, "I might as well warn you that Diane Carter has called three times this morning. I told her you were coming in late and I didn't expect you before ten. Brace yourself. I have a feeling she'll be calling back, or better yet, she'll be coming up here the first chance she gets."

"Thanks for the warning."

Renee was about to go into her office when Vicki asked, "Did you enjoy yourself last night?"

Renee met the woman's gaze. She saw genuine concern and interest in the eyes staring back at her. Nothing judgmental and no censorship. "Yes, I had a wonderful time."

Vicki smiled. "I'm glad. You're a beautiful woman, Renee, and a nice person. You should get out more and enjoy yourself."

Renee lifted a brow. "And Teagan Elliott?"

Vicki shrugged. "I don't know him personally, but he seems like a nice young man." She glanced back down at the newspaper that was still spread open on her desk. "And no matter how anyone else might feel, I personally think the two of you look wonderful together."

Renee smiled, not realizing she'd been holding her breath. One thing she knew about Vicki was that she was sincere and forthright. "Thanks, Vicki." She then walked into her office and closed the door.

It was sometime after the lunch hour when Diane burst into Renee's office. "Vicki wasn't out front so I just came on in. This is the first chance I've had to sneak away since seeing today's paper. What on earth were you thinking about by going out with Teagan Elliott? That was definitely not a smart move, Renee."

Renee leaned back in her chair, deciding to give Diane credit. The woman definitely didn't have a problem expressing the way she felt. "And why would you think that?"

Diane frowned. "Surely you're joking. Come on, Renee, walk back into the real world. People like the Elliotts don't become involved with people like us. We're not on their social level and with you it's even more serious. There's the issue of—"

"Race?" She preempted Diane's comment.

"Yes, that's it." Diane smiled apologetically. "Face it. You're probably a novelty to him, something new and different. I hope you aren't taking things seriously because if you are you're setting yourself up to get hurt."

"Thanks for the warning, Diane, but I'm a big girl and I can take care of myself." She reached for a file on her desk, hoping Diane would take the hint.

Diane's smile slipped. "I hope so because you'll need to be strong when he loses interest and drops you like a hot potato. If I were you that would be something I'd definitely be thinking about."

Without saying anything else, Diane turned and walked out of Renee's office.

Renee stood at the window and looked down at the busy streets below. The lunch hour had ended a while ago but the sidewalks were still crowded.

Preferring to have lunch alone in her office, Renee had eaten a sandwich her secretary had brought up from the cafeteria.

She sighed deeply. She hadn't wanted to fall in love with Tag for several reasons, and this was one of them. She hated being the center of attention, detested her name being linked to office gossip. It brought back so many painful memories of when Dionne had humiliated her in the worst possible way.

She tried convincing herself that the talk about her and Tag wasn't the same, but in her mind, talk was talk, and she'd rather not have her name linked to any of it.

She tensed when she heard the phone ring and hoped it wasn't Tag. She hadn't heard from him all day and wondered if he had seen the pictures.

She crossed the room and picked up the phone. "Yes, Vicki?"

"Ms. Elliott is on the line for you."

Renee raised a brow. "Ms. Elliott?"

"Yes, Ms. Bridget Elliott."

Renee swallowed. Tag's siblings had been friendly to her last night but she couldn't help wondering if they saw the photographs in today's paper as damaging to their family name. "Please put her through, Vicki."

For the next minute Renee exchanged pleasantries with Tag's sister. Then Bridget surprised her by asking, "I was wondering if we could have lunch tomorrow?"

"Lunch?"

"Yes, tomorrow. We could meet somewhere near the hospital. How about Carmine's, that Italian restaurant on Broadway? Say noon?"

Renee took a step around her desk to quickly check her calendar. Finding the time open, she said, "Noon will be fine."

Once Renee ended the call she slumped down in her chair. Was Bridget inviting her to lunch to tell her that she thought Renee seeing Tag was a bad idea? The last thing she needed was another person criticizing her relationship with Tag.

Tag gazed at the special edition of *Pulse*. On the front cover was the silhouette of Senator Denton highlighted by the words—emblazoned in bold, black letters—"Silence is Not Always Golden".

Tag rubbed his hand down his face. *Pulse* had obtained undisputed proof that one of the military guards at Abu Ghraib Prison had written the Senator and had sent photographs about the abuse going on, but Senator Denton had failed to do anything about it, and had gone so far as to stage a cover-up by having the informer transferred to a military outfit in the heart of the Iraqi fighting. That same individual had gotten killed within days of being put on the front line.

Although the incident at Abu Ghraib had eventually been brought to light, Senator Denton's actions had not. The plan had been for him to quietly resign from office before anyone could discover the truth. Luckily, his niece had overheard him giving orders to one of his staffers to destroy the letters and photographs, and before anyone could do so, she'd read them. Horrified, she'd decided to expose her uncle for the dishonest person that he was. The loss of that young marine's life couldn't be forgiven.

Tag glanced down at his watch. It was close to 10 p.m. He'd been in the office since nine that morning, after finally forcing himself from Renee's bed and going home to shower and change.

Leaning back in his chair, he threw down the magazine and picked up that day's newspaper, a copy of which Gannon had placed on his desk first thing that morning. Tag had smiled when he'd seen the pictures of him and Renee, thinking how good they looked together. He had reached for the phone several times to call her to make sure she'd known about the photographs, but each time he'd gotten interrupted.

It was probably too late to call her now but he'd speak to her tomorrow. In the midst of everything that was going on, he needed to hear her voice and to know that the pictures hadn't bothered her.

He gazed at the photographs and could distinctly remember when they had gotten out of the limo together, as well as the exact moment he had placed a kiss on her lips at the ball. He hadn't been aware that the latter was being captured on film but a part of him didn't care. There was nothing wrong with a man displaying affection for the woman he loved.

The woman he loved.

Thinking it, realizing it and accepting it was easier than he'd ever imagined. He loved her and more than anything he wanted to find a way to make her love him as well, and believe that things between them would work out.

"I can't believe she actually thinks Teagan Elliott is remotely interested in her."

"Hey, isn't that hilarious? I heard that Diane Carter tried to warn her but she refused to listen. She's going to wish she had when she gets dumped. It won't be anyone's fault but her own."

Renee kept walking, refusing to look over her shoulder to see who was speaking. A part of her wanted to turn around and tell whoever they were just where they could go, but she was too professional. Besides, it would be a waste of time since the remarks were bits and pieces of what she'd heard all day, thanks to Diane's handiwork. She sighed, thinking that the one thing she had hoped would never happen to her again was happening. Once again, she was the topic of everyone's conversations.

She stepped into the elevator, glad she was leaving the building even if it was only for a little while. She hoped she didn't later regret agreeing to meet Tag's sister for lunch. Although Tag had told her that he'd be too tied up at the office to call, a part of her wished he had so she'd know what he thought of the pictures.

She'd contemplated calling him but knew how busy he was. She, like everyone else, had seen the special edition of *Pulse*, and had been shocked to read the article about Senator Denton. It had been the hot topic on the subway that morning.

Her thoughts shifted to her conversation with Diane yesterday. Last night, while lying in bed, she'd been forced to acknowledge that Diane was probably right. Eventually, Tag would lose interest and Renee couldn't help wondering where that would leave her heart. Probably somewhere shattered into a million pieces. Could she handle such heartbreak?

As she stepped outside onto the sidewalk she tightened her coat around her. No, she wasn't a glutton for pain, and if she didn't make decisions about their relationship before Tag eventually did, pain would be just what she got.

When Renee walked into Carmine's, she was surprised to not only see Bridget but Tag's identical twin cousins, Summer and Scarlet, as well. She had met the two women at the Valentine's Day ball. She nervously gripped the straps of her purse as the host led her across the room to join them.

"Thanks for inviting me to lunch," Renee said with the first real smile she'd managed in a couple of days, after being greeted with genuine friendliness by the three women.

Bridget grinned. "It was supposed to be the two of us, but then I ran into Summer and Scarlet at the office and invited them along. I hope you don't mind, but Summer has a good reason for us to celebrate," Bridget said, picking up her wineglass.

Renee glanced over at Summer and quickly saw the reason. A beautiful engagement ring adorned the fourth finger of her left hand. "Congratulations! It's a beautiful ring."

Summer returned Renee's smile. "Thanks. John proposed to me on Valentine's Day. We only made a brief appearance at the ball since he'd made dinner reservations elsewhere. That's when he popped the question."

"Have you set a date?" Renee asked, lifting her own glass of wine after the waiter came and filled it.

She wondered then if she was the only one who noted how Summer's shoulders had tensed at that question.

"No, a date hasn't been set yet," the bride-to-be replied.

Renee nodded and took a sip of wine, thinking Summer didn't appear to be as pleased with her engagement as a future bride should be. She set down her wineglass, deciding to leave Summer's issue alone since Renee had a huge one of her own. Tag. She wondered how long it would take before Bridget brought him up.

An hour later they had eaten their meal, and still Tag's sister hadn't mentioned him. Instead, she talked about how improved her mother's condition was and had asked questions as to what to expect during Karen's chemotherapy treatment. Tag's name never came up. Instead, Renee spent an enjoyable lunch getting to know his sister and cousins.

It was only when they were leaving the restaurant that Bridget leaned over, smiled and whispered to Renee, "Oh, and by the way, I thought you and Tag looked great together at the ball as well as in yesterday's paper."

Eleven

The following day Renee walked into her apartment not in the best of moods. The stares and negative comments at work had been worse than ever today and she wasn't sure tonight would be a good time to go out with Tag. She had spoken to him briefly that day before he'd gotten interrupted by someone coming into his office.

On the subway ride home she had replayed everything she'd had to endure for the past two days. She had been so concerned about what everyone was saying and thinking that she hadn't been able to function at work. That kind of worry and aggravation would definitely put a strain on an already difficult relationship and she was beginning to feel it.

More than ever she was convinced that their differences would always be an issue with them.

She glanced at her watch. Tag was to pick her up at seven, and knowing him, he would be punctual. If she was going to cancel their date, now was the time to do so. She picked up the phone, deciding to call him at the office in case he was still there. The familiar voice of his secretary answered after the first couple of rings. "Teagan Elliott's office."

"Yes, may I speak with Mr. Elliott?"

"He's in a meeting right now. Would you like to leave a message?"

"Yes. Please let him know that Renee Williams called and—"

"Hold on, Ms. Williams. I was given explicit instructions to put you through to Mr. Elliott if you were to call. Just a moment, please."

Renee leaned back against the kitchen counter, waiting to be connected to Tag. A few seconds later, he was on the line. "Renee?"

She sucked in a sharp breath. Just hearing him say her name did things to her. She could vividly remember how he'd woken her a couple of mornings ago, kissing her and whispering her name over and over. Before she'd even opened her eyes, he'd drawn her into his warm embrace, waking her senses up to him and the strong evidence of his desire for her.

Could Diane be right? Was she just a novelty to him? Something different? Someone he would eventually lose interest in when the novelty wore off? And what if she did mean something to him? Would he go against his family's wishes if they decided they didn't want her to be a part of it? Could there ever be a chance of a happy ending for them?

"Renee?"

She breathed in deeply. "Yes, it's me. I called to let you know I don't think it's a good idea for us to go out tonight. And maybe it's a good idea if we cool things between us."

"What are you talking about, Renee? What happened?"

"Nothing happened, Tag. I—I just can't handle the talk, the negativity. Look, I know you're busy so I'll let you go. Goodbye."

She hung up the phone and wrapped her arms around her stomach, swallowing her tears, telling herself that she wouldn't fall apart. But when the tears continued coming nonstop, she knew she was doing that exact thing.

Tag held the phone in his hand as he hung his head, frowning. What the hell had happened? He breathed in deeply, knowing whatever it was had to be connected to the pictures that had appeared in the newspaper a few days ago.

"Is everything all right, Tag?"

He glanced up and met Gannon's concerned gaze. Only then did he hang up the phone. Already, he was moving toward the coatrack for his jacket. "No, everything isn't all right. It's Renee and she's having second thoughts about us again." Last night while the two of them were stuck late at the office, Tag had had a heart-to-heart talk to Gannon about Renee, and had even admitted to his brother that he loved her.

"Maybe it's time for you to erase those thoughts from her mind forever or they're going to just keep coming back."

Tag sighed disgustedly. "And how am I supposed to

do that if she keeps letting what people say come between us?"

"Then it's up to you to convince her it doesn't matter. If you love her as much as you say you do, then you'll find a way to convince her."

Tag nodded. "I hate to run out on you like this but I need to go see Renee."

"By all means, go and do whatever it takes to win your lady's heart."

Tag was grateful for his brother's support. "If anything further develops with the Denton story, call me on my cell phone," he said, rushing toward the door while slipping on his jacket. "I'll talk with you later."

Renee should have assumed Tag would show up, and if she'd been in her right frame of mind, she would have. But she wasn't, so when the doorbell sounded she fought to get her tears under control. Wiping the evidence off her cheeks, she took a deep breath before crossing the room to answer the door.

She immediately met Tag's gaze and saw the anger in the depths of his eyes, which she tried meeting with complete serenity in hers, knowing she was failing. There was no way he wouldn't know she'd been crying.

"May I come in?"

Instead of answering, she took a step back and watched as he crossed the threshold then closed the door behind him. "We need to talk, Renee," he said softly, slipping a hand under her chin to stare into her puffy eyes.

The tears she was holding back threatened to fall

with his sudden shift from anger to tenderness. "There's nothing to say, Tag," she said simply. "We gave it a try and it didn't work."

"No, you gave up too soon."

Fire suddenly sparked in Renee at his accusation. She stiffened. "I'm sorry you feel that way but people are talking about us and I don't appreciate being the topic of gossip at work. They're probably taking bets like the last time."

"I don't give a damn what people are—" He suddenly stopped talking and lifted a brow. "What do you mean they're probably taking bets like the last time? What last time?"

Renee could have kicked herself for letting that comment slip out. "Nothing."

He gazed at her with intensity. "No, I think it *is* something, so tell me."

Renee looked away from his face. Maybe she needed to do what he was asking and tell him about Dionne and why she had moved from Atlanta. Only then would he understand why being in the midst of a scandal bothered her so much. "Let's sit down. You're right. It is time I tell you."

When he started to sit beside her on the sofa she quickly said, "No. Please sit over there." She indicated the chair across from the sofa. She wasn't certain of her control and needed space from Tag. She couldn't handle things if he were to sit beside her, touch her, breathe on her.

He stared at her for a few moments before doing as she asked. As soon as he was settled he met her gaze and waited for her to speak.

She curled up on the sofa, tucking her feet under her. "Before I came to New York I worked at a hospital in Atlanta and dated this doctor for almost a year before finding out he was also dating a nurse who worked the midnight shift. She didn't know about me like I didn't know about her but some of the other doctors knew and were taking bets as to when I would find out. Eventually I did and it was the talk of the hospital. It seemed everywhere I went there were whispers, looks of pity, even laughter. The embarrassment was humiliating. When I came here I promised myself that I would never get involved in any situation where I was the center of attention again. But it seems, once again, that I am."

Tag didn't say anything but stared at her, and Renee knew he was trying to formulate in his mind just what to say. "I regret what your ex-boyfriend did to you, Renee, but I'm not him," he said in a quiet voice. "I am not involved with anyone but you."

She sighed slowly. "That's not why people are talking and you know it."

"Okay, then, let's discuss why people are talking."

"No," she said softly, knotting her hands together in her lap. "We already have, numerous times, and you won't accept how it makes me feel."

He leaned forward and held her gaze. "Then maybe we need to discuss why the talk makes you feel that way in the first place," he said calmly. "Why you can't get beyond the color of my skin and the amount of money in my bank account." He continued speaking in a calm voice. "And before you answer, I want you to know how I feel about you, Renee. I love you. I think I fell in love with you that first day in your office. I want a future with you. A very happy future."

With his admission of love, tears Renee couldn't hold back any longer began flowing down her cheeks. Fighting for composure, she spoke straight from her heart. "And I love you, too, Tag. I didn't want to fall in love with you but I did that very same day as well. But that's just it. We can't have the happy future you want. All I can see is a future filled with the strain of proving our love to the world, constantly defending it, working harder than most couples just to preserve it. Then what if we want children? What will they have to go through?"

Tag got to his feet and crossed to the sofa. He reached out and took Renee's hand and gently pulled her up. "So what if our challenges will be greater than most? Our love will be there to sustain us. And as far as children are concerned, they'll grow up proud of what they are and who they are. Times have changed, Renee. And they are still changing. There will always be people who are bitterly opposed to interracial marriages, but then you'll find there's an even larger number of people who see such unions as an indicator of what life will be like in an even more diverse twenty-first century."

"Dammit, Tag, I can't bank on an unknown future. I can only go by what's in the real world, now."

Both fury and pain flashed in Tag's eyes. "So you're saying that you can't accept me or my love because it will be a problem for others to accept it? Are you saying that you're willing to give up what we can have together because of how others think and feel? What about how we feel, Renee? Is that not equally important?"

"Yes, it's important, but can't you understand that I'm trying to protect you, as well? I heard whispers at the ball of how your grandfather would be against anything developing between us, and I refuse to be the cause of any rift between you and your family."

His face hardened. "I told you that how my family might feel about us didn't matter to me, so don't go there, Renee. Don't look for excuses."

He released her and took a step back. "I don't know what else I can say. I love you. I want to marry you. I want a future with you," he said quietly, feeling the strain of heartbreak and disappointment. "That is what you have to believe and what you have to accept. My wanting those things means nothing unless you want them as well. All I'm asking is for us to put our love to the test and tell anyone who can find any reason for us not to be together to go straight to hell and stay there."

"Tag, I don't think—"

"No," he said, cutting her off, struggling to contain his anger. "The bottom line is whether you're strong enough to step out on faith and love. A week from today is my brother's wedding at The Tides as well as my grandparents' anniversary celebration. I want you to go there with me, not to seek any type of approval from my family but as two individuals who are very much in love and who have committed their lives to each other, and who are ready to make an announcement regarding their future together."

Renee shook her head sadly as tears once again filled

her eyes. In a voice filled with frustration, she said, "I can't do that, Tag. I'm sorry, but I can't."

And before he could say anything else, she rushed to her bedroom and slammed the door.

Twelve

Renee whirled around. Her face was streaked with tears, her eyes swollen and tormented. "What do you mean you think I'm making a mistake?"

Debbie Massey met her best friend's glare as she handed her a wet washcloth. "Renee, you know me well enough to know I don't sugarcoat anything. You asked for my honest opinion so I gave it to you."

Debbie, who'd been out of the country on assignment, had shown up at Renee's place over an hour ago and found Renee still torn up over her dealings with Tag the night before. With a bossiness that Renee doubted she would ever get used to, Debbie had quickly taken charge and rushed Renee off to the bathroom, made her wash her face while she'd told Debbie everything.

"Didn't you hear anything I said regarding all the

problems Tag and I would be facing as an interracial couple? How can you say I'm making a mistake?"

"The same way you did when I broke things off with Alan last year. I didn't follow my heart and I've regretted it every day since."

Renee nodded. Alan Harris, a colleague of Debbie's, was fifteen years her senior. Concerned about what others would say about her dating a much older man, Debbie had ended their relationship after a brief affair. That had been over a year ago and this was the first time Renee had heard Debbie admit that maybe she'd made a mistake in letting Alan go.

Before she could ask questions, Debbie continued. "At some point in your life you have to do what makes *you* happy and not worry about how others may feel about it. You've admitted you're in love with Teagan Elliott and he has admitted that he's in love with you. He's a man— a wealthy one, I might add—who wants to marry you and make you happy. If only the rest of us could be so lucky."

Renee dropped into a chair at the kitchen table, struggling to control the tears that threatened to fall again. "But you weren't around to hear what everyone was saying once they saw those pictures of us."

Debbie frowned. "And it's a good thing I wasn't. People need to get their own lives and not worry about what's going on in other people's lives. It's time you stopped caring about what people are saying and thinking. No matter what, you won't be able to change their opinion about anything, so why bother? They are either accepting or they aren't."

Debbie then tossed the braids out of her face and

peered at Renee over her glasses. "But none of what I'm telling you means a thing if you don't love Tag Elliott as much as you claim you do."

"I do love him," Renee said fiercely. "I love him with all my heart."

"Then act like it. There was a time you used to fight for what you wanted, what you believed in. I remember that day in college when Professor Downey gave you a B and you felt that you deserved an A. Where I would have taken the B and been giddy about it—being that it was a physics class—you didn't give the man a day's rest until he recalculated your scores to discover he'd made a mistake. You got your A and proved your point. Maybe it's time for you to prove another point, Renee. You, and only you, can decide your destiny."

Renee sipped her coffee as she thought about Debbie's words. She then asked, "Have you decided on your destiny, Debbie?"

Her friend smiled. "I think I have. It just so happens that Alan was in London while I was there. The moment I saw him I knew I still loved him. We were able to spend some time together and I've decided that I'm not going to let what others think stand in the way of my happiness. Maybe you ought to be making the same decision."

"Hey, you okay?"

Tag glanced up from his coffee cup and met Gannon's concerned gaze. It was Saturday morning and they had come into the office to take a conference call from Senator Denton's office. There would be a press conference from the Senator's home at noon where he would admit that *Pulse*'s allegations were true.

The special edition of *Pulse* had flown off the magazine stands and already there had been another printing, so there was indeed a reason to celebrate. Both their father and grandfather—who'd returned to town that morning—had called to congratulate them on a job well done. The only sad note was that Gannon had to advise Peter that he would no longer be associated with the company. After all the man's years of dedicated service the decision had been hard, but necessary.

"Yes, I'm all right," Tag replied, running a hand down his face. Next week was his brother's wedding and the last thing he wanted Gannon to worry about was him. "Are you nervous about the wedding next week?" he decided to ask.

Gannon chuckled. "No, just anxious. I can hardly wait."

Tag nodded. "And have you decided where you're going on your honeymoon yet?"

"Yes, but I'm keeping it as a surprise to Erika. I'm taking her to Paris."

"That's going to be some surprise."

Gannon calmly sipped his coffee and after a few moments of silence he said over the rim of his mug, "I didn't ask how things went with you and Renee last night but I get the feeling they didn't go as you wanted. Let me give you a word of advice, kiddo. No matter what, don't let her go without a fight. If you love her as much as I think you do, you'll be making a big mistake if you give up on her."

Tag dragged a hand through his hair. "It's not me giving up on her, Gannon. It's Renee giving up on me. She knows that I love her. It will be up to her to decide if my love is worth all the challenges we might face in the future." He let out a long breath and added, "And it's my most fervent hope that she does."

By Wednesday, Renee was still trying to get her life back in order. So far, work had gone smoothly. Instead of whispering about her and Tag, everyone focused on the scandal involving Senator Denton and the press conference he'd held that weekend where he'd admitted all of *Pulse*'s allegations.

She sighed as she caught the elevator to the tenth floor to visit with one of her patients. For the past five days she had replayed in her mind, over and over, her conversation with Debbie, and it didn't help matters that she was missing Tag like crazy. She thought of him all the time and missed the good times they had shared together.

She let out a long breath. Nobody could make her see the errors of her ways more thoroughly than Debbie and she appreciated her friend for doing that. Since their talk, she'd been thinking of how a future with Tag would be versus one without him, and each time the thought of a life without him was too heart wrenching to imagine. She refused to let what others thought make her lose the best thing that had ever happened to her. She loved Tag and he loved her and together they would be able to handle anything. She smiled to herself, thinking that later tonight she planned to pay him a visit and let him know just how she felt.

Renee had stepped off the elevator and was about to

round the corner when she heard the sound of Diane's voice. "Yes, she's been hiding out in her office, totally embarrassed. I would be embarrassed, too, if I had thrown myself at Teagan Elliott of all people. Maybe now she's learned to stay in her place. The nerve of her thinking she could cross over to the other side, and not just with anyone but with a member of one of the wealthiest families in New York. Can you imagine anyone being that stupid?"

Anger consumed Renee and she squared her shoulders and continued walking, remembering her last conversation with Tag and some of the advice he'd given her. Diane's back was to Renee, and the other nurse with whom Diane had been conversing saw Renee over Diane's shoulders. The nurse quickly made an excuse and hurried off, leaving Diane alone.

"Diane?"

The woman whirled around, surprised to find Renee standing there. She raised a brow. "Yes?"

"Do me a favor."

Diane relaxed and had the audacity to smile. "Sure, Renee, what do you need?"

"For you to go straight to hell and stay there."

Renee moved past the woman and then thought of something else, and turned around and added, "And the only stupid thing I've done was not accept Tag's marriage proposal."

Satisfied with the shocked look on Diane's face, Renee turned and resumed walking with her head held high. She couldn't go around telling everyone to go to hell like Tag had suggested, but she felt good about telling Diane to.

* * *

Tag rose from the sofa to turn off the television. It didn't matter that the Knicks were on a winning streak, even the basketball game wasn't holding his interest. The only thing consuming his mind were thoughts of Renee.

Renee.

More than once he had wondered if there was anything else he could have said to make her accept the love he was offering. He needed her in his life like he needed to breathe, and the pain of her willingness to give up and walk away was killing him.

He glanced around when the doorbell sounded, thinking it was probably Liam dropping by. As much as he loved his brother, Tag wasn't in the mood for company.

Opening the door he said, "Liam, I don't think—"

The words died on his lips when he saw it wasn't Liam like he'd assumed, but it was Renee.

"Hi," she said, smiling tentatively at him. "May I come in?"

A part of Tag was so glad to see her that he wanted to reach out and pull her into his arms but he knew he couldn't. He wasn't sure why she'd come but he did know there were still unresolved issues between them and until they worked them out, they were still at odds with each other.

"Sure, you can come in," he said, taking a step back to let her inside. He closed the door behind her. "May I take your coat?"

"Yes, thanks."

He watched her slide the leather coat from her body

to reveal a beautiful turquoise sweater and a pair of black slacks. Both looked good on her. "Can I get you something to drink?" he asked, taking the coat she handed him.

"No, I'm fine."

He nodded and walked over to the coat closet to hang up her coat. He could feel the tension in the air and could tell that her nerves were jumping just as high as his. "It's good seeing you, Renee," he said when he walked back over to her.

"Thanks, and it's good seeing you, too. I was wondering if we could talk."

He nodded. "Sure, let's sit in the living room."

He waited until she sat down on the sofa and then, remembering her request the last time they'd talked, he took the chair opposite her.

Renee crossed her legs, feeling Tag's penetrating stare. Over the past five days she had done a lot of soul-searching and had made a lot of decisions, and she wanted to share them with him.

"Are you sure I can't get you anything to drink?"

"No, I'm fine." Then a few moments later she said, "No, that's a lie and I'm not fine." She stood and slowly began pacing the room. Tag said nothing as he watched her and she knew he was giving her time to collect her thoughts.

"I don't know where to begin," she finally said, coming to a stop not far from where he sat and meeting his concentrated gaze.

"I know one place you can start," he said calmly, soothingly and in a low voice. "You can start off by assuring me that you meant what you said Friday night. The part about being in love with me."

His words were spoken with such tenderness that Renee's lips began trembling. How could she not love such a man as this? And that was only one of the things she intended to reassure him about. "Yes, I meant what I said, Tag. I do love you and I will always love you… which leads me to the reason I'm here."

She took a step back, needing to say what she had to say without being tempted to lean down and kiss him like she wanted to do. That would come later if he still wanted her. "I thought about everything you said that night and I've made some decisions."

"You have?"

"Yes."

"And what decisions have you made?" he quietly probed.

She met his gaze. "If you still want me, if you still love me, then I'm willing to do whatever it takes to make a future work with you, Tag. I'm no longer worried or concerned about what others might say. All I care about is what my heart is saying, and right now it's telling me that you're the best thing to ever happen to me and that you are the one person I need in my life. Now and forever."

She reclaimed the step she'd taken earlier to stand in front of him. She reached out, grabbed his hands and gently pulled him from his chair. "I know things won't always be easy. I know there will be those not happy with us being together, but as long as we have each other, then it won't matter. Our love will be strong enough to handle anything. I truly believe that now. I want to marry you, Tag. I want to have a future with you. I want to have your babies. I want it all."

Tag smiled, let out a relieved sigh and pulled Renee into his arms. "Thank you for reaching that decision. And yes, I still want you and I love you. I will always love you, Renee. And I want to marry you, have a future with you, have babies with you to grow and nurture in our love. I—"

Renee smiled and instead of letting him speak, she stood on tiptoe and touched her mouth to his. Tag, needing the kiss as much as she did, began hungrily devouring her mouth the moment they connected. He reached out, gathered her closer and molded her body to his, desperately needing the feel of her in his arms, close to his heart.

She slid a hand to his shoulder, holding on, fighting for control of the emotions he was stirring to life inside of her. Renee groaned as his tongue relentlessly mated with hers, claiming, absorbing everything about him.

And when the kiss grew more heated and demanding, he lifted her into his arms and whispered, "I want to make love to you."

The kiss had aroused her, too, and thoughts of being naked in bed with him, joining her body with his and sealing their love once and for all had her whispering back, "I want to make love to you, too."

Tag headed for the bedroom and within minutes her wish came true. They were naked in bed, and Tag was staring at her with love shining in the depths of his eyes. When he reached into the drawer to get a condom, she stopped him. "There's no need unless you want to do that. I've been on the pill for a couple of years to regulate my periods."

He met her gaze and tossed the packet back in the drawer. "I've never made love to a woman without using a condom," he decided to admit to her. "But I'm aching to do so with you. And just so you know, I'm safe. Because it's one of EPH's policies, I take physicals on a regular basis."

Returning to the bed, he whispered, "I love you with all my heart," just moments before leaning down, moving his body in place over hers and taking her lips in a slow, sensuous exchange, deliberately stimulating her senses as he slowly entered her, merging their bodies into one, flesh to flesh.

Tag's presence back inside her body evoked such pleasure in Renee that she lifted her hips and wrapped her legs around his waist, not wanting him to go anyplace but here, locked to her. Desire as powerful as anything she could imagine began consuming her, filling her mind with all kinds of sensations, and of their own accord, her eyes drifted close.

"Open your eyes, sweetheart," Tag urged in a low, raspy voice. "Look at me and tell me what you see."

Renee complied with his request and looked up at him, taking in his handsome face, the majestic blue of his eyes and the long lashes covering them. Her inner muscles quaked just from looking at him.

She reached up and skimmed a fingertip along his lips, taking in the mouth that could drive her out of her mind. "What I see when I look at you," she whispered, "is a man who is my soul mate, my fantasy come true, the only man I love and want to spend the rest of my life with, the future father of my babies."

Tag's breath caught with Renee's words. She was so beautiful, captivating…and she was his. "I love you so much," he murmured, before capturing her mouth. He began moving the lower part of his body, feeling the hardened tips of her breasts against his chest.

He established a rhythm and began moving inside her to a beat only the two of them could hear. And then it happened. He threw his head back as a release of gigantic proportions tore out of him. He screamed her name as he relinquished his entire being to passion of the richest and most intense kind. And to the woman he loved.

As if the feel of him coming apart, exploding inside of her, was what she wanted, she followed him over the edge. "I don't believe this," she sighed at the peak of her pleasure. She cried out his name and bucked upward, tightening her legs around him.

"Believe it, baby," he whispered. "This is just the beginning of the rest of our lives together. Forever."

As more sensations tore into Renee's body, the only thing she could do was meet his gaze and agree. "Yes. Forever."

Epilogue

"**R**enee, I'm glad you came," Karen Elliott said, smiling, grasping Renee's hand in hers.

Renee returned the woman's smile. "I'm glad I came, too." She glanced around. It seemed Gannon and Erika's wedding, although it had been done on a small scale, still had numerous invited guests. Everything had been beautiful; especially the bride, and tears had touched Renee's eyes when she'd seen the depth of love shining in Gannon's gaze for Erika.

She glanced up at Tag. They had decided to marry next year on Valentine's Day since that day was so special to them. It was almost a year away but it would be worth the wait. They had decided to announce their intentions to only his parents and grandparents tonight since it was Gannon and Erika's day. But when the couple returned from their honeymoon, Tag and Renee planned to make an official announcement to everyone.

"Where have Dad and Granddad run off to?" Tag inquired of his mother. He had remained at Renee's side throughout the entire wedding, always touching her in some way, making it known, just in case anyone had any doubt, that she was special to him.

Karen glanced around. "Probably in the library. Why?"

"I need to speak with them and I want you and Grandmother included in the conversation."

Karen's smile widened. "All right, let me go get Maeve and we'll meet you there in a few minutes."

When Karen walked off, the smile Tag gave Renee was reassuring, absolute. "You okay?" he asked, meeting her gaze, detecting some nervousness there.

She smiled back at him. "Yes, how can I not be? I'm in love with a wonderfully amazing man and what's so truly magnificent is that he loves me, too."

"Always," Tag whispered, taking her hand and lifting it to his lips. "Let's go congratulate Gannon and Erika in case we don't get a chance to do so later."

Renee nodded. What Tag wasn't saying and what she knew nonetheless, was that after telling his grandparents and parents about their plans, if anyone seemed the least bit not pleased, he intended to leave. He had meant what he'd said about not tolerating anything but total acceptance from his grandfather regarding their future marriage.

A part of Renee wasn't sure they would get it. She had seen the look in Patrick Elliott's eyes the moment Tag had walked into the room with her. Tag's grandmother had displayed a genuine open friendliness when introductions had been made moments before the start of the wedding. But Patrick Elliott had been standoffish. Tag had gotten the same vibes and had placed a protective hand around her waist, reiterating silently that he didn't need, nor was he seeking, his grandfather's approval.

Tag and Renee walked into the library sometime later. A Victorian-style chandelier hung from the ceiling, illuminating the elegance of the stylish room. Tag had told her when they'd pulled into the estate from the private road that the entire house had been lovingly decorated by his grandmother.

"I understand you wanted to speak with us, Tag," Patrick Elliott said in a deep, gruff voice. Renee studied him. Tall, distinguished-looking, with a medium build, he actually looked at least ten years younger than the age Tag had claimed his grandfather to be. His hair was completely gray and his eyes were the same shade of blue as Tag's. And the one thing she noted was that there wasn't a hint of a smile on his face.

"Yes, I have an announcement to make," Tag said, holding Renee's hand and closing the door behind them. His parents were sitting on a gray sofa and looked at them expectantly. Tag's grandmother was sitting in a chair within a few feet of where Patrick stood with one elbow resting on the mantel of a massive fireplace.

"And just what is this announcement?" Patrick asked.

Tag met Renee's eyes and smiled. "I just wanted all of you to know that I love Renee very much and I've asked her to marry me, and she has agreed to do so next year on Valentine's Day."

Tag's parents, as well as his grandmother, immediately hugged the couple and offered words of congratulations. However, a quick glance at Patrick indicated he hadn't moved an inch and there was a stunned, frozen look etched on his features. "Marriage?" he finally asked, his deep voice drowning out everyone else's. "Are the two of you sure that is what you want to do?"

Tag's hand tightened around Renee's waist. "Yes. Marriage is precisely what we want and what we plan to do," he said, meeting his grandfather's gaze.

It was quite obvious that Patrick wasn't ecstatic with the news, and it was just as apparent that Tag wasn't letting his grandfather's lack of joy influence him in any way.

"I'll be telling the rest of the family when Gannon and Erika return from their honeymoon, but I wanted the four of you to know now."

It was Tag's grandmother, who knew her husband better than anyone, who decided the best thing to do was to make sure Patrick gave his blessing. She went to her husband. "Aye, 'tis a night to celebrate. On our anniversary day one of our grandsons got married and another announced his engagement to a very beautiful young woman. 'Tis a bit special, don't you think, Patrick?"

Patrick met his wife's gaze and everyone knew the woman that he loved more than anything was daring him to contradict her. He only hesitated for a brief moment before lifting her hand to his lips and saying. "Yes, darling, it is special."

Leaving his wife's side, he went to stand before the

couple. "I wish the two of you the best," he said, shaking Tag's hand and then pulling Renee to him in a hug.

"Welcome to the family, Renee," he said in a voice that was still somewhat gruff. "And after this wedding takes place I fully expect you and Tag to start working on some great-grandchildren for me and Maeve to enjoy while we still can."

He took a step back. "Now we need to return to the wedding reception, which will be followed by Maeve's and my anniversary party." Without saying anything else, he walked out of the room.

Later than night Renee lay in Tag's arms, their limbs tangled, their bodies naked, after having just made love. She sighed with pleasure as well as contentment. Gannon and Erika's wedding had been beautiful and the anniversary party that followed for Tag's grandparents had been nothing short of exquisite.

"Are you sure you want us to wait until next February?" Tag asked, leaning over and nibbling at her ear. "That's a long time from now."

Renee smiled as she tilted her head back. "It's less than a year, but I'll find a way to keep you busy until then…not like you don't already have enough to do at work. At least by our wedding the feud between the different magazines will be over and behind everyone."

Tag nodded, looking forward to that day. "How about a big wedding at The Tides?"

Renee grinned. The suggestion definitely appealed to her. She had fallen in love with his grandparents' home. "I think that's a wonderful idea," she said, leaning up and touching her lips to his. "And of course we'll let your mother plan everything."

Tag chuckled. "Of course."

Renee's smile faded somewhat when she said, "Your grandfather hasn't accepted the idea of our marriage one hundred percent, Tag."

Tag met her gaze. "No, but that's his problem and not ours," he said fiercely. "However, I have a feeling that by the day of our wedding he will have come around. And if not, then oh, well. Nothing, and I mean nothing, is going to stop me from making you an Elliott a year from now."

With a smile, Renee leaned up and kissed him. "I like your determination."

"You do?" he asked. "And what else do you like?"

She reached down and her fingers found him hard, large and ready again. "Um, I definitely like the way you go about taking care of business," she said, shifting her body to let him know what she wanted and needed.

He leaned down and kissed her, and responding to him was so natural she took everything he was offering and more. And when he straddled her body and slowly eased inside of her, her mind went blank except for one thought. Yes, she definitely liked the way he was taking care of business.

* * * * *

Don't miss the next exciting title in THE ELLIOTTS.
Pick up CAUSE FOR SCANDAL
by Anna DePalo this March.

From reader-favorite

Kathie DeNosky

THE ILLEGITIMATE HEIRS

A brand-new miniseries about three
brothers denied a father's name, but
granted a special inheritance.

Don't miss:

Engagement
between Enemies

(Silhouette Desire #1700,
on sale January 2006)

Reunion
of Revenge

(Silhouette Desire #1707,
on sale February 2006)

Betrothed
for the Baby

(Silhouette Desire #1712,
on sale March 2006)

If you enjoyed what you just read,
then we've got an offer you can't resist!

Take 2 bestselling love stories FREE!

Plus get a FREE surprise gift!

Clip this page and mail it to Silhouette Reader Service™

IN U.S.A.	**IN CANADA**
3010 Walden Ave.	P.O. Box 609
P.O. Box 1867	Fort Erie, Ontario
Buffalo, N.Y. 14240-1867	L2A 5X3

YES! Please send me 2 free Silhouette Desire® novels and my free surprise gift. After receiving them, if I don't wish to receive anymore, I can return the shipping statement marked cancel. If I don't cancel, I will receive 6 brand-new novels every month, before they're available in stores! In the U.S.A., bill me at the bargain price of $3.80 plus 25¢ shipping and handling per book and applicable sales tax, if any*. In Canada, bill me at the bargain price of $4.47 plus 25¢ shipping and handling per book and applicable taxes**. That's the complete price and a savings of at least 10% off the cover prices—what a great deal! I understand that accepting the 2 free books and gift places me under no obligation ever to buy any books. I can always return a shipment and cancel at any time. Even if I never buy another book from Silhouette, the 2 free books and gift are mine to keep forever.

225 SDN DZ9F
326 SDN DZ9G

Name	(PLEASE PRINT)	
Address	Apt.#	
City	State/Prov.	Zip/Postal Code

Not valid to current Silhouette Desire® subscribers.

Want to try two free books from another series?
Call 1-800-873-8635 or visit www.morefreebooks.com.

* Terms and prices subject to change without notice. Sales tax applicable in N.Y.
** Canadian residents will be charged applicable provincial taxes and GST.
   All orders subject to approval. Offer limited to one per household.
   ® are registered trademarks owned and used by the trademark owner and or its licensee.

DES04R   ©2004 Harlequin Enterprises Limited

WHAT HAPPENS IN VEGAS...

Shock! Proud casino owner
Hayden MacKenzie's former fiancée,
who had left him at the altar for a cool
one million dollars, was back in Sin City.
It was time for the lovely Shelby Paxton
to pay in full—starting with the wedding
night they never had....

His Wedding-Night Wager

by Katherine Garbera

On sale February 2006 (SD #1708)

Also look for:

Her High-Stakes Affair, March 2006
Their Million-Dollar Night, April 2006

COMING NEXT MONTH

#1711 CAUSE FOR SCANDAL—Anna DePalo
The Elliotts
She posed as her identical twin and bedded a rock star—now the
shocking truth is about to be revealed!

#1712 BETROTHED FOR THE BABY—Kathie DeNosky
The Illegitimate Heirs
What happens when coworkers playing husband and wife begin
wishing they were betrothed for real?

#1713 TOTALLY TEXAN—Mary Lynn Baxter
He's the total Texan package and she's just looking for a little
rest and relaxation…. Sounds perfect—until their hearts get
involved.

#1714 HER HIGH-STAKES AFFAIR—Katherine Garbera
What Happens in Vegas…
An affair between them is forbidden, but all bets are off when
passion strikes under the neon lights of Vegas!

#1715 A SPLENDID OBSESSION—Cathleen Galitz
She was back in town to get her life together…not fall for a man
who dared her to be his inspiration.

#1716 SECRETS IN THE MARRIAGE BED—Nalini Singh
Will an unplanned pregnancy save a severed marriage and
rekindle a love that's been stifled for five years?

SDCNM0206